THE EARLY BIRD
A Business Man's
Love Story

by

George Randolph Chester

Double 9
BOOKS

THE EARLY BIRD
A Business Man's Love Story
by George Randolph Chester

Copyright © 2023

All Rights reserved.

ISBN: 978-93-57488-22-8

Published by

DOUBLE 9 BOOKS
2/13-B, Ansari Road
Daryaganj, New Delhi – 110002
info@double9books.com
www.double9books.com
Tel. 011-40042856

ABOUT THE AUTHOR

George Randolph Chester was an American author, screenwriter, film editor, and director. He was born on January 27, 1869, and died on February 26, 1924. Chester was born on January 27, 1869, in Cincinnati, Ohio. He wrote popular books like Get-Rich-Quick Wallingford and Five Thousand an Hour: How Johnny Gamble Won the Heiress, both of which were turned into silent movies while he was still alive. James Bearsley Hendryx decided to try his hand at writing fiction after he had success selling stories to The Saturday Evening Post. This led him to quit his job at the Cincinnati Enquirer and move to New York City to write fiction. Elizabeth Chester, who was George Chester's first wife, got a divorce from him in 1911 because he was living with Lillian Josephine Chester at Gainsborough Studios in London. George and Lillian collaborated on a number of stories and plays. The Son of Wallingford (1921), which has been lost, was the only movie that George and Lillian made together. Chester died of a heart attack in his New York City home on February 26, 1924.

CONTENTS

CHAPTER I.
WHEREIN A VERY BUSY YOUNG MAN STARTS ON AN ABSOLUTE REST

The youngish-looking man who so vigorously swung off the train at Restview, wore a pair of intensely dark blue eyes which immediately photographed everything within their range of vision—flat green country, shaded farm-houses, encircling wooded hills and all—weighed it and sorted it and filed it away for future reference; and his clothes clung on him with almost that enviable fit found only in advertisements. Immediately he threw his luggage into the tonneau of the dingy automobile drawn up at the side of the lonely platform, and promptly climbed in after it. Spurred into purely mechanical action by this silent decisiveness, the driver, a grizzled graduate from a hay wagon, and a born grump, as promptly and as silently started his machine. The crisp and perfect start, however, was given check by a peremptory voice from the platform.

"Hey, you!" rasped the voice. "Come back here!"

As there were positively no other "Hey yous" in the landscape, the driver and the alert young man each acknowledged to the name, and turned to see an elderly gentleman, with a most aggressive beard and solid corpulency, gesticulating at them with much vigor and earnestness. Standing beside him was a slender sort of girl in a green outfit, with very large brown eyes and a smile of amusement which was just a shade mischievous. The driver turned upon his passenger a long and solemn accusation.

"Hollis Creek Inn?" he asked sternly.

"Meadow Brook," returned the passenger, not at all abashed, and he smiled with all the cheeriness imaginable.

"Oh," said the driver, and there was a world of disapprobation in his tone, as well as a subtle intonation of contempt. "You are not Mr. Stevens of Boston."

"No," confessed the passenger; "Mr. Turner of New York. I judge that to be Mr. Stevens on the platform," and he grinned.

The driver, still declining to see any humor whatsoever in the situation, sourly ran back to the platform. Jumping from his seat he opened the door of the tonneau, and waited with entirely artificial deference for Mr. Turner of New York to alight. Mr. Turner, however, did nothing of the sort. He merely stood up in the tonneau and bowed gravely.

"I seem to be a usurper," he said pleasantly to Mr. Stevens of Boston. "I was expected at Meadow Brook, and they were to send a conveyance for me. As this was the only conveyance in sight I naturally supposed it to be mine. I very much regret having discommoded you."

He was looking straight at Mr. Stevens of Boston as he spoke, but, nevertheless, he was perfectly aware of the presence of the girl; also of her eyes and of her smile of amusement with its trace of mischievousness. Becoming conscious of his consciousness of her, he cast her deliberately out of his mind and concentrated upon Mr. Stevens. The two men gazed quite steadily at each other, not to the point of impertinence at all, but nevertheless rather absorbedly. Really it was only for a fleeting moment, but in that moment they had each penetrated the husk of the other, had cleaved straight down to the soul, had estimated and judged for ever and ever, after the ways of men.

"I passed your carryall on the road. It was broke down. It'll be here in about a half hour, I suppose," insisted the driver, opening the door of the tonneau still wider, and waving the descending pathway with his right hand.

Both Mr. Stevens of Boston and Mr. Turner of New York were very glad of this interruption, for it gave the older gentleman an object upon which to vent his annoyance.

"Is Meadow Brook on the way to Hollis Creek?" he demanded in a tone full of reproof for the driver's presumption.

The driver reluctantly admitted that it was.

"I couldn't think of leaving you in this dismal spot to wait for a dubious carryall," offered Mr. Stevens, but with frigid politeness. "You are quite welcome to ride with us, if you will."

"Thank you," said Mr. Turner, now climbing out of the machine with alacrity and making way for the others. "I had intended," he laughed, as he took his place beside the driver, "to secure just such an invitation, by hook or by crook."

For this assurance he received a glance from the big eyes; not at all a flirtatious glance, but one of amusement, with a trace of mischief. The remark, however, had well-nigh stopped all conversation on the part of Mr. Stevens, who suddenly remembered that he had a daughter to protect, and must discourage forwardness. His musings along these lines were interrupted by an enthusiastic outburst from Mr. Turner.

"By George!" exclaimed the latter gentleman, "what a fine clump of walnut trees; an even half-dozen, and every solitary one of them would trim sixteen inches."

"Yes," agreed the older man with keenly awakened interest, "they are fine specimens. They would scale six hundred feet apiece, if they'd scale an inch."

"You're in the lumber business, I take it," guessed the young man immediately, already reaching for his card-case. "My name is Turner, known a little better as Sam Turner, of Turner and Turner."

"Sam Turner," repeated the older man thoughtfully. "The name seems distinctly familiar to me, but I do not seem, either, to remember of any such firm in the trade."

"Oh, we're not in the lumber line," replied Mr. Turner. "Not at all. We're in most anything that offers a profit. We—that is my kid brother and myself—have engineered a deal or two in lumber lands, however. It was only last month that I turned a good trade—a very good trade—on a tract of the finest trees in Wisconsin."

"The dickens!" exclaimed the older gentleman explosively. "So you're the Turner who sold us our own lumber! Now I know you. I'm Stevens, of the Maine and Wisconsin Lumber Company."

Sam Turner laughed aloud, in both surprise and glee. Mr. Stevens had now reached for his own card-case. The two gentlemen exchanged cards, which, with barely more than a glance, they poked in the other flaps of their cases; then they took a new and more interested inspection of each other. Both were now entirely oblivious to the girl, who, however, was by no means oblivious to them. She found them, in this new meeting, a most interesting study.

"You gouged us on that land, young man," resumed Mr. Stevens with a wry little smile.

"Worth every cent you paid us for it, wasn't it?" demanded the other.

"Y-e-s; but if you hadn't stepped into the deal at the last minute, we could have secured it for five or six thousand dollars less money."

"You used to go after these things yourself," explained Mr. Turner with an easy laugh. "Now you send out people empowered only to look and not to purchase."

"But what I don't yet understand," protested Mr. Stevens, "is how you came to be in the deal at all. When we sent out our men to inspect the trees they belonged to a chap in Detroit. When we came to buy them they belonged to you."

"Certainly," agreed the younger man. "I was up that way on other business, when I heard about your man looking over this valuable acreage; so I just slipped down to Detroit and hunted up the owner and bought it. Then I sold it to you. That's all."

He smiled frankly and cheerfully upon Mr. Stevens, and the frown of discomfiture which had slightly clouded the latter gentleman's brow, faded away under the guilelessness of it all; so much so that he thought to introduce his daughter.

Miss Josephine having been brought into the conversation, Mr. Turner, for the first time, bent his gaze fully upon her, giving her the same swift scrutiny and appraisement that he had the father. He was evidently highly satisfied with what he saw, for he kept looking at it as much as he dared. He became aware after a moment or so that Mr. Stevens was saying something to him. He never did get all of it, but he got this much:

"—so you'd be rather a good man to watch, wherever you go."

"I hope so," agreed the other briskly. "If I want anything, I go prepared to grab it the minute I find that it suits me."

"Do you always get everything you want?" asked the young lady.

"Always," he answered her very earnestly, and looked her in the eyes so speculatively, albeit unconsciously so, that she found herself battling with a tendency to grow pink.

Her father nodded in approval.

"That's the way to get things," he said. "What are you after now? More lumber?"

"Rest," declared Mr. Turner with vigorous emphasis. "I've worked like a nailer ever since I turned out of high school. I had to make the living for the family, and I sent my kid brother through college. He's just been out a year and it's a wonder the way he takes hold. But do you know that in all those times since I left school I never took a lay-off until just this minute? It feels glorious already. It's fine to look around this good stretch of green country and breathe this fresh air and look at those hills over yonder, and to realize that I don't have to think of business for two solid weeks. Just absolute rest, for me! I don't intend to talk one syllable of shop while I'm here. Hello! there's another clump of walnut trees. It's a pity they're scattered so that it isn't worth while to buy them up."

The girl laughed, a little silvery laugh which made any memory of grand opera seem harsh and jangling. Both men turned to her in surprise. Neither of them could see any cause for mirth in all the fields or sky.

"I beg your pardon for being so silly," she said; "but I just thought of something funny."

"Tell it to us," urged Mr. Turner. "I've never taken the time I ought to enjoy funny things, and I might as well begin right now."

But she shook her head, and in some way he acquired an impression that she was amused at him. His brows gathered a trifle. If the young lady intended to make sport of him he would take her down a peg or two. He would find her point of susceptibility to ridicule, and hammer upon it until she cried enough. That was his way to make men respectful, and it ought to work with women.

When they let him out at Meadow Brook, Mr. Stevens was kind enough to ask him to drop over to Hollis Creek. Mr. Turner, with impulsive alacrity, promised that he would.

CHAPTER II.
WHEREIN MR. TURNER PLUNGES INTO THE BUSINESS OF RESTING

At Meadow Brook Sam Turner found W. W. Westlake, of the Westlake Electric Company, a big, placid man with a mild gray eye and an appearance of well-fed and kindly laziness; a man also who had the record of having ruthlessly smashed more business competitors than any two other pirates in his line. Westlake, unclasping his fat hands from his comfortable rotundity, was glad to see young Turner, also glad to introduce the new eligible to his daughter, a girl of twenty-two, working might and main to reduce a threatened inheritance of embonpoint. Mr. Turner was charmed to meet Miss Westlake, and even more pleased to meet the gentleman who was with her, young Princeman, a brisk paper manufacturer variously quoted at from one to two million. He knew all about young Princeman; in fact, had him upon his mental list as a man presently to meet and cultivate for a specific purpose, and already Mr. Turner's busy mind offset the expenses of this trip with an equal credit, much in the form of "By introduction to H. L. Princeman, Jr. (Princeman and Son Paper Mills, AA 1), whatever it costs." He liked young Princeman at sight, too, and, proceeding directly to the matter uppermost in his thoughts, immediately asked him how the new tariff had affected his business.

"It's inconvenient," said Princeman with a shake of his head. "Of course, in the end the consumers must pay, but they protest so much about it that they disarrange the steady course of our operations."

"It's queer that the ultimate consumer never will be quite reconciled to his fate," laughed Mr. Turner; "but in this particular case, I think I hold the solution. You'll be interested, I know. You see—"

"I beg your pardon, Mr. Turner," interrupted Miss Westlake gaily; "I know you'll want to meet all the young folks, and you'll particularly want to meet my very dearest friend. Miss Hastings, Mr. Turner."

Mr. Turner had turned to find an extraordinarily thin young woman, with extraordinarily piercing black eyes, at Miss Westlake's side.

"Indeed, I do want to meet all the young people," he cordially asserted, taking Miss Hastings' claw-like hand in his own and wondering what to do with it. He could not clasp it and he could not shake it. She relieved him of his dilemma, after a moment, by twining that arm about the plump waist of her dearest friend.

"Is this your first stay at Meadow Brook?" she asked by way of starting conversation. She was very carefully vivacious, was Miss Hastings, and had a bird-like habit, meant to be very fetching, of cocking her head to one side as she spoke, and peering up to men—oh, away up—with the beady expression of a pet canary.

"My very first visit," confessed Mr. Turner, not yet realizing the disgrace it was to be "new people" at Meadow Brook, where there was always an aristocracy of the grandchildren of original Meadow Brookers. "However, I hope it won't be the last time," he continued.

"We shall all hope that, I am certain," Miss Westlake assured him, smiling engagingly into the depths of his eyes. "It will be our fault if you don't like it here;" and he might take such tentative promise as he would from that and her smile.

"Thank you," he said promptly enough. "I can see right now that I'm going to make Meadow Brook my future summer home. It's such a restful place, for one thing. I'm beginning to rest right now, and to put business so far into the background that—" he suddenly stopped and listened to a phrase which his trained ear had caught.

"And that is the trouble with the whole paper business," Mr. Princeman was saying to Mr. Westlake. "It is not the tariff, but the future scarcity of wood-pulp material."

"That's just what I was starting to explain to you," said Mr. Turner, wheeling eagerly to Mr. Princeman, entirely unaware, in his intensity of interest, of his utter rudeness to both groups. "My kid brother and myself are working on a scheme which, if we are on the right track, ought to bring about a revolution in the paper business. I can not give you the exact details of it now, because we're waiting for letters patent on it, but the fundamental point is this: that the wood-pulp manufacturers within a few years will have to grow their raw material, since wood is becoming so scarce and so high priced. Well, there is any quantity of swamp land available, and we have experimented like mad with reeds and rushes. We've found one particular variety which grows very rapidly, has a strong, woody fiber, and makes the finest pulp in the world. I turned the kid loose with the company's bank roll this spring, and he secured options on two thousand acres of swamp land, near to transportation and particularly adapted to this culture, and dirt cheap because it is useless for any other purpose. As soon as the patents are granted on our process we're going to organize a million dollar stock company to take up more land and handle the business."

"Come over here and sit down," invited Princeman, somewhat more than courteously.

"Wait a minute until I send for McComas. Here, boy, hunt Mr. McComas and ask him to come out on the porch."

The new guest was reaching for pencil and paper as they gathered their chairs together. The two girls had already started hesitantly to efface themselves. Half-way across the lawn they looked sadly toward the porch again. That handsome young Mr. Turner, his back toward them, was deep in formulated but thrilling facts, while three other heads, one gray and one black and one auburn, were bent interestedly over the envelope upon which he was figuring.

Later on, as he was dressing for dinner, Mr. Turner decided that he liked Meadow Brook very much. It was set upon the edge of a pleasant, rolling valley, faced and backed by some rather high hills, upon the sloping side of one of which the hotel was built, with broad verandas looking out upon exquisitely kept flowers and shrubbery and upon the shallow little brook which gave the place its name. A little more water would have suited Sam better, but the management had made the most of its opportunities, especially in the matter of arranging dozens of pretty little lovers' lanes leading in all directions among the trees and along the sides of the shimmering stream, and the whole prospect was very good to look at, indeed. Taken in conjunction with the fact that one had no business whatever on hand, it gave one a sense of delightful freedom to look out on the green lawn and the gay gardens, on the brook and the tennis and croquet courts, and on the purple-hazed, wooded hills beyond; it was good to fill one's lungs with country air and to realize for a little while what a delightful world this is; to see young people wandering about out there by twos and by threes, and to meet with so many other people of affairs enjoying leisure similar to one's own.

Of course, this wasn't a really fashionable place, being supported entirely by men who had made their own money; but there was Princeman, for instance, a fine chap and very keen; a well-set-up fellow, black-haired and black-eyed, and of a quick, nervous disposition; one of precisely the kind of energy which Turner liked to see. McComas, too, with his deep red hair and his tendency to freckles, and his frank smile with all the white teeth behind it, was a corking good fellow; and alive. McComas was in the furniture line, a maker of cheap stuff which was shipped in solid trains of carload lots from a factory that covered several acres. The other men he noticed around the place seemed to be of about the same stamp. He had never been anywhere that the men averaged so well.

As he went down-stairs, McComas introduced his wife, already gowned for the evening. She was a handsome woman, of the sort who would wear a different stunning gown every night for two weeks and then go on to the next place. Well, she had a right to this extravagance. Besides it is good for a man's business to have his wife dressed prosperously. A man who is getting on in the world ought to have a handsome wife. If she is the right kind, of Miss Stevens' type, say, she is a distinct asset.

After dinner, Miss Westlake and Miss Hastings waylaid him on the porch.

"I suppose, of course, you are going to take part in the bowling tournament to-night," suggested Miss Westlake with the engaging directness allowable to family friendship.

"I suppose so, although I didn't know there was one. Where is it to be held?"

"Oh, just down the other side of the brook, beyond the croquet grounds. We have a tournament every week, and a prize cup for the best score in the season. It's lots of fun. Do you bowl?"

"Not very much," Mr. Turner confessed; "but if you'll just keep me posted on all these various forms of recreation, you may count on my taking a prominent share in them."

"All right," agreed Miss Hastings, very vivaciously taking the conversation away from Miss Westlake. "We'll constitute ourselves a committee of two to lay out a program for you."

"Fine," he responded, bending on the fragile Miss Hastings a smile so pleasant that it made her instantly determine to find out something about his family and commercial standing. "What time do we start on our mad bowling career?"

"They'll be drifting over in about a half-hour," Miss Westlake told him, with a speculative sidelong glance at her dearest girl friend. "Everybody starts out for a stroll in some other direction, as if bowling was the least of their thoughts, but they all wind up at the alleys. I'll show you." A slight young man of the white-trousered faction, as distinguished from the dinner-coat crowd, passed them just then. "Oh, Billy," called Miss Westlake, and introduced the slight young man, who proved to be her brother, to Mr. Turner, at the same time wreathing her arm about the waist of her dear companion.

"Come on, Vivian; let's go get our wraps," and the girls, leaving "Billy" and Mr. Turner together, scurried away.

The two young men looked at each other dubiously, though each had an earnest desire to please. They groped for human understanding, and suddenly that clammy, discouraged feeling spread its muffling wall between them. Billy was the first to recover in part.

"Charming weather, isn't it?" he observed with a polite smile.

Mr. Turner opined that it was, the while delving into Mr. Westlake's mental workshop and finding it completely devoid of tools, patterns or lumber.

"The girls are just going to take me over to bowl," Mr. Turner ventured desperately after a while. "Do you bowl very much?"

"Oh, I usually fill in," stated Mr. Westlake; "but really, I'm a very poor hand at it. I seem to be a poor hand at most everything," and he laughed with engaging candor, as if somehow this were creditable.

The conversation thereupon lagged for a moment or two, while Mr. Turner blankly asked himself: "What in thunder *does* a man talk about when he has nothing to say and nobody to say it to?" Presently he solved the problem.

"It must be beautiful out here in the autumn," he observed.

"Yes, it is indeed," returned Mr. Westlake with alacrity. "The leaves turn all sorts of colors."

Once more conversation lagged, while Billy feebly wondered how any person could possibly be so dull as this chap. He made another attempt.

"Beastly place, though, when it rains," he observed.

"Yes, I should imagine so," agreed Mr. Turner. Great Scott! The voice of McComas saved him from utter imbecility.

"You'll excuse Mr. Turner a moment, won't you, Billy?" begged McComas pleasantly. "I want to introduce him to a couple of friends of mine."

Billy Westlake bowed his forgiveness of Mr. McComas with fully as much relief as Sam Turner had felt. Over in the same corner of the porch where he had sat in the afternoon with McComas and Princeman and the elder Westlake, Sam found awaiting them Mr. Cuthbert, of the American Papier-Mâché Company, an almost viciously ugly man with a twisted nose and a crooked mouth, who controlled practically all the worth-while papier-mâché business of the United States, and Mr. Blackrock, an elderly man with a young toupee and particularly gaunt cheek-bones, who was a corporation lawyer of considerable note. Both gentlemen greeted Mr. Turner as one toward whom they were already highly predisposed, and Mr. Princeman and Mr. Westlake also shook hands most cordially, as if Sam had been gone for a day or two. Mr. McComas placed a chair for him.

"We just happened to mention your marsh pulp idea, and Mr. Cuthbert and Mr. Blackrock were at once very highly interested," observed McComas as they sat dawn. "Mr. Blackrock suggests that he don't see why you need wait for the issuance of the letters patent, at least to discuss the preliminary steps in the forming of your company."

"Why, no, Mr. Turner," said Mr. Blackrock, suavely and smoothly; "it is not a company anyhow, as I take it, which will depend so much upon letters patent as upon extensive exploitation."

"Yes, that's true enough," agreed Sam with a smile. "The letters patent, however, should give my kid brother and myself, without much capital, controlling interest in the stock."

Upon this frank but natural statement the others laughed quite pleasantly.

"That seems a plausible enough reason," admitted Mr. Westlake, folding his fat hands across his equator and leaning back in his chair with a placidity which seemed far removed from any thought of gain. "How did you propose to organize your company?"

"Well," said Sam, crossing one leg comfortably over the other, "I expect to issue a half million participating preferred stock, at five per cent., and a half-million common, one share of common as bonus with each two shares of preferred; the voting power, of course, vested in the common."

A silence followed that, and then Mr. Cuthbert, with a diagonal yawing of his mouth which seemed to give his words a special dryness, observed:

"And I presume you intend to take up the balance of the common stock?"

"Just about," returned Mr. Turner cheerfully, addressing Cuthbert directly. The papier-mâché king was another man whom he had inscribed, some time since, upon his mental list. "My kid brother and myself will take two hundred and fifty thousand of the common stock for our patents and processes, and for our services as promoters and organizers, and will purchase enough of the preferred to give us voting power; say five thousand dollars worth."

Mr. Cuthbert shook his head.

"Very stringent terms," he observed. "I doubt if you will interest your capital on that basis."

"All right," said Sam, clasping his knee in his hands and rocking gently. "If we can't organize on that basis we won't organize at all. We're in no hurry.

My kid brother's handling it just now, anyhow. I'm on a vacation, the first I ever had, and not keen upon business, by any means. In the meantime, let me show you some figures."

Five minutes later, Billy Westlake and his sister and Miss Hastings drew up to the edge of the group. Young Westlake stood diffidently for two or three minutes beside Mr. Turner's chair, and then he put his hand on that summer idler's shoulder.

"Oh, good evening, Mr.—Mr.—Mr.—" Sam stammered while he tried to find the name.

"Westlake," interposed Billy's father; and then, a trifle impatiently, "What do you want, Billy?"

"Mr. Turner was to go over with us to the bowling shed, dad."

"That's so," admitted Mr. Turner, glancing over to the porch rail where the girls stood expectantly in their fluffy white dresses, and nodding pleasantly at them, but not yet rising. He was in the midst of an important statement.

"Just you run on with the girls, Billy," ordered Mr. Westlake. "Mr. Turner will be over in a few minutes."

The others of the circle bent their eyes gravely upon Billy and the girls as they turned away, and waited for Mr. Turner to resume.

At a quarter past ten, as Mr. Turner and Mr. Princeman walked slowly along the porch to turn into the parlors for a few minutes of music, of which Sam was very fond, a crowd of young people came trooping up the steps. Among them were Billy Westlake and his sister, another young gentleman and Miss Hastings.

"By George, that bowling tournament!" exclaimed Mr. Turner. "I forgot all about it."

He was about to make his apologies, but Miss Westlake and Miss Hastings passed right on, with stern, set countenances and their heads in air. Apparently they did not see Mr. Turner at all. He gazed after them in consternation; suddenly there popped into his mind the vision of a slender girl in green, with mischievous brown eyes—and he felt strangely comforted. Before retiring he wired his brother to send some samples of the marsh pulp, and the paper made from it.

CHAPTER III.
MR. TURNER APPLIES BUSINESS PROMPTNESS TO A MATTER OF DELICACY

Morning at Meadow Brook was even more delightful than evening. The time Mr. Turner had chosen for his outing was early September, and already there was a crispness in the air which was quite invigorating. Clad in flannels and with a brand new tennis racket under his arm, he went into the reading-room immediately after breakfast, bought a paper of the night before and glanced hastily over the news of the day, paying more particular attention to the market page. Prices of things had a peculiar fascination for him. He noticed that cereals had gone down, that there was another flurry in copper stock, and that hardwood had gone up, and ranging down the list his eye caught a quotation for walnut. It had made a sharp advance of ten dollars a thousand feet.

Out of the window, as he looked up, he saw Miss Westlake and Miss Hastings crossing the lawn, and he suddenly realized that he was here to wear himself out with rest, so he hurried in the direction the girls had taken; but when he arrived at the tennis court he found a set already in progress. Both Miss Westlake and Miss Hastings barely nodded at Mr. Turner, and went right on displaying grace and dexterity to a quite unusual degree. Decidedly Mr. Turner was being "cut," and he wondered why. Presently he strode down to the road and looked up over the hill in the direction he knew Hollis Creek Inn to be. He was still pondering the probable distance when Mr. Westlake and Billy and young Princeman came up the brook path.

"Just the chap I wanted to see, Sam," said Mr. Westlake heartily. "I'm trying to get up a pin-hook fishing contest, for three-inch sunfish."

"Happy thought," returned Sam, laughing. "Count me in."

"It's the governor's own idea, too," said Billy with vast enthusiasm. "Bully sport, it ought to be. Only trouble is, Princeman has some mysterious errand or other, and can't join us."

"No; the fact is, the Stevenses were due at Hollis Creek yesterday," confessed Mr. Princeman in cold return to the prying Billy, "and I think I'll stroll over and see if they've arrived."

Sam Turner surveyed Princeman with a new interest. Danger lurked in Princeman's black eyes, fascination dwelt in his black hair, attractiveness was in every line of his athletic figure. It was upon the tip of Sam's tongue to say that he would join Princeman in his walk, but he repressed that instinct immediately.

"Quite a long ways over there by the road, isn't it?" he questioned.

"Yes," admitted Princeman unsuspectingly, "it winds a good bit; but there is a path across the hills which is not only shorter but far more pleasant."

Sam turned to Mr. Westlake.

"It would be a shame not to let Princeman in on that pin-hook match," he suggested. "Why not put it off until to-morrow morning. I have an idea that I can beat Princeman at the game."

There was more or less of sudden challenge in his tone, and Princeman, keen as Sam himself, took it in that way.

"Fine!" he invited. "Any time you want to enter into a contest with me you just mention it."

"I'll let you know in some way or other, even if I don't make any direct announcement," laughed Sam, and Princeman walked away with Mr. Westlake, very much to Billy's consternation. He was alone with this dull Turner person once more. What should they talk about? Sam solved that problem for him at once. "What's the swiftest conveyance these people keep?" he asked briskly.

"Oh, you can get most anything you like," said Billy. "Saddle-horses and carriages of all sorts; and last year they put in a couple of automobiles, though scarcely any one uses them." There was a certain amount of careless contempt in Billy's tone as he mentioned the hired autos. Evidently they were not considered to be as good form as other modes of conveyance.

"Where's the garage?" asked Sam.

"Right around back of the hotel. Just follow that drive."

"Thanks," said the other crisply. "I'll see you this evening," and he stalked away leaving Billy gasping for breath at the suddenness of Sam. After all, though, he was glad to be rid of Mr. Turner. He knew the Stevenses himself, and it had slowly dawned on him that by having his own horse saddled he could beat Princeman over there.

It took Sam just about one minute to negotiate for an automobile, a neat little affair, shiny and new, and before they were half-way to Hollis Creek, his innate democracy led him into conversation with the driver, an alert young man of the near-by clay.

"Not very good soil in this neighborhood," Sam observed. "I notice there is a heavy outcropping of stone. What are the principal crops?"

"Summer resorters," replied the driver briefly.

"And do you mean to tell me that all these farm-houses call themselves summer resorts?" inquired Sam.

"No, only those that have running water. The others just keep boarders."

"I see," said Sam, laughing.

A moment later they passed over a beautifully clear stream which ran down a narrow pocket valley between two high hills, swept under a rickety wooden culvert, and raced on across a marshy meadow, sparkling invitingly here and there in the sunlight.

"Here's running water without a summer resort," observed the passenger, still smiling.

"It's too much shut in," replied the chauffeur as one who had voiced a final and insurmountable objection. All the "summer resorts" in this neighborhood were of one pattern, and no one would so much as dream of varying from the first successful model.

Sam scarcely heard. He was looking back toward the trough of those two picturesquely wooded hills, and for the rest of the drive he asked but few questions.

At Hollis Creek, where he found a much more imposing hotel than the one at Meadow Brook, he discovered Miss Stevens, clad in simple white from canvas shoes to knotted cravat, in a summer-house on the lawn, chatting gaily with a young man who was almost fat. Sam had seen other girls since he had entered the grounds, but he could not make out their features; this one he had recognized from afar, and as they approached the summer-house he opened the door of the machine and jumped out before it had come properly to a stop.

"Good morning, Miss Stevens," he said with a cheerful self-confidence which was beautiful to behold. "I have come over to take you a little spin, if you'll go."

Miss Stevens gazed at the caller quizzically, and laughed outright.

"This is so sudden," she murmured.

The caller himself grinned.

"Does seem so, if you stop to think of it," he admitted. "Rather like dropping out of the clouds. But the auto is here, and I can testify that it's a smooth-running machine. Will you go?"

She turned that same quizzical smile upon the young man who was almost fat, and introduced him, curly hair and all, to Mr. Turner as Mr. Hollis, who, it afterward transpired, was the heir to Hollis Creek Inn.

"I had just promised to play tennis with Mr. Hollis," Miss Stevens stated after the introduction had been properly acknowledged, "but I know he won't mind putting it off this time," and she handed him her tennis bat.

"Certainly not," said young Hollis with forcedly smiling politeness.

"Thank you, Mr. Hollis," said Sam promptly. "Just jump right in, Miss Stevens."

"How long shall we be gone?" she asked as she settled herself in the tonneau.

"Oh, whatever you say. A couple of hours, I presume."

"All right, then," she said to young Hollis; "we'll have our game in the afternoon."

"With pleasure," replied the other graciously, but he did not look it.

"Where shall we go?" asked Sam as the driver looked back inquiringly. "You know the country about here, I suppose."

"I ought to," she laughed. "Father's been ending the summer here ever since I was a little girl. You might take us around Bald Hill," she suggested to the chauffeur. "It is a very pretty drive," she explained, turning to Sam as the machine wheeled, and at the same time waving her hand gaily to the disconsolate Hollis, who was "hard hit" with a different girl every season. "It's just about a two-hour trip. What a fine morning to be out!" and she settled back comfortably as the machine gathered speed. "I do love a machine, but father is rather backward about them. He will consent to ride in them under necessity, but he won't buy one. Every time he sees a handsome pair of horses, however, he has to have them."

"I admire a good horse myself," returned Sam.

"Do you ride?" she asked him.

"Oh, I have suffered a few times on horseback," he confessed; "but you ought to see my kid brother ride. He looks as if he were part of the horse. He's a handsome brat."

"Except for calling him names, which is a purely masculine way of showing affection, you speak of him almost as if you were his mother," she observed.

"Well, I am, almost," replied Sam, studying the matter gravely. "I have been his mother, and his father, and his brother, too, for a great many years; and I will say that he's a credit to his family."

"Meaning just you?" she ventured.

"Yes, we're all we have; just yet, at least." This quite soberly.

"He must talk of getting married," she guessed, with a quick intuition that when this happened it would be a blow to Sam.

"Oh, no," he immediately corrected her. "He isn't quite old enough to think of it seriously as yet. I expect to be married long before he is."

Miss Stevens felt a rigid aloofness creeping over her, and, having a very wholesome sense of humor, smiled as she recognized the feeling in herself.

"I should think you'd spend your vacation where the girl is," she observed. "Men usually do, don't they?"

He laughed gaily.

"I surely would if I knew the girl," he asserted.

"That's a refreshing suggestion," she said, echoing his laugh, though from a different impulse. "I presume, then, that you entertain thoughts of matrimony merely because you think you are quite old enough."

"No, it isn't just that," he returned, still thoughtfully. "Somehow or other I feel that way about it; that's all. I have never had time to think of it before, but this past year I have had a sort of sense of lonesomeness; and I guess that must be it."

In spite of herself Miss Josephine giggled and repressed it, and giggled again and repressed it, and giggled again, and then she let herself go and laughed as heartily as she pleased. She had heard men say before, but always with more or less of a languishing air, inevitably ridiculous in a man, that they thought it about time they were getting married; but she could not remember anything to compare with Sam Turner's naïveté in the statement.

He paid no attention to the laughter, for he had suddenly leaned forward to the chauffeur.

"There is another clump of walnut trees," he said, eagerly pointing them out. "Are there many of them in this locality?"

"A good many scattered here and there," replied the boy; "but old man Gifford has a twenty-acre grove down in the bottoms that's mostly all walnut trees, and I heard him say just the other day that walnut lumber's got so high he had a notion to clear his land."

"Where do you suppose we could find old man Gifford?" inquired Mr. Turner.

"Oh, about six miles off to the right, at the next turning."

"Suppose we whizz right down there," said Sam promptly, and he turned to Miss Stevens with enthusiasm shining in his eyes. "It does seem as if everything happens lucky for me," he observed. "I haven't any particular liking for the lumber business, but fate keeps handing lumber to me all the time; just fairly forcing it on me."

"Do you think fate is as much responsible for that as yourself?" she questioned, smiling as they passed at a good clip the turn which was to have taken them over the pretty Bald Hill drive. Sam had not even thought to apologize for the abrupt change in their program, because she could certainly see the opportunity which had offered itself, and how imperative it was to embrace it. The thing needed no explanation.

"I don't know," he replied to her query, after pausing to consider it a moment. "I certainly don't go out of my road to hunt up these things."

"No-o-o-o," she admitted. "But fate hasn't thrust this particular opportunity upon me, although I'm right with you at the time. It never would have occurred to me to ask about those walnut trees."

"It would have occurred to your father," he retorted quickly.

"Yes, it might have occurred to father, but I think that under the circumstances he would have waited until to-morrow to see about it."

"I suppose I might be that way when I arrive at his age," Sam commented philosophically, "but just now I can't afford it. His 'seeing about it to-morrow' cost him between five and six thousand dollars the last time I had anything to do with him."

She laughed. She was enjoying Sam's company very much. Even if a bit startling, he was at least refreshing after the type of young men she was in the habit of meeting.

"He was talking about that last night," she said. "I think father rather stands in both admiration and awe of you."

"I'm glad to hear that," he returned quite seriously. "It's a good attitude in which to have the man with whom you expect to do business."

"I think I shall have to tell him that," she observed, highly amused. "He will enjoy it, and it may put him on his guard."

"I don't mind," he concluded after due reflection. "It won't hurt a particle. If anything, if he likes me so far, that will only increase it. I like your father. In fact I like his whole family."

"Thank you," she said demurely, wondering if there was no end to his bluntness, and wondering, too, whether it were not about time that she should find it wearisome. On closer analysis, however, she decided that the time was not yet come. "But you have not met all of them," she reminded him. "There are mother and a younger sister and an older brother."

"Don't matter if there were six more, I like all of them," Sam promptly informed her. Then, "Stop a minute," he suddenly directed the chauffeur.

That functionary abruptly brought his machine to a halt just a little way past a tree glowing with bright green leaves and red berries.

"I don't know what sort of a tree that is," said Sam with boyish enthusiasm; "but see how pretty it is. Except for the shape of the leaves the effect is as beautiful as holly. Wouldn't you like a branch or two, Miss Stevens?"

"I certainly should," she heartily agreed. "I don't know how you discovered that I have a mad passion for decorative weeds and things."

"Have you?" he inquired eagerly. "So have I. If I had time I'd be rather ashamed of it."

He had scrambled out of the car and now ran back to the tree, where, perching himself upon the second top rail of the fence he drew down a limb, and with his knife began to snip off branches here and there. The girl noticed that he selected the branches with discrimination, turning each one over so that he could look at the broad side of it before clipping, rejecting many and studying each one after he had taken it in his hand. He was some time in finding the last one, a long straggling branch which had most of its leaves and berries at the tip, and she noticed that as he came back to the auto he was arranging them deftly and with a critical eye. When he handed them in to her they formed a carefully arranged and graceful composition. It was a new and an unexpected side of him, and it softened considerably the amused regard in which she had been holding him.

"They are beautifully arranged," she commented, as he stopped for a moment to brush the dust from his shoes in the tall grass by the roadside.

"Do you think so?" he delightedly inquired. "You ought to see my kid brother make up bouquets of goldenrod and such things. He seems to have a natural artistic gift."

She bent on his averted head a wondering glance, and she reflected that often this "hustler" must be misunderstood.

"You have aroused in me quite a curiosity to meet this paragon of a brother," she remarked. "He must be well-nigh perfection."

"He is," replied Sam instantly, turning to her very earnest eyes. "He hasn't a flaw in him any place."

She smiled musingly as she surveyed the group of branches she held in her hand.

"It is a pity these leaves will wither in so short a time," she said.

"Yes," he admitted; "but even if we have to throw them away before we get back to the hotel, their beauty will give us pleasure for an hour; and the tree won't miss them. See, it seems as perfect as ever."

"It wouldn't if everybody took the same liberties with it that you did," she remarked, glancing back at the tree.

Sam had climbed in the car and had slammed the door shut, but any reply he might have made was prevented by a hail from the woods above them at the other side of the road, and a man came scrambling down from the hillside path.

"Why, it's Mr. Princeman!" exclaimed the girl in pleased surprise. "Think of finding you wandering about, all alone in the woods here."

"I wasn't wandering about," he protested as he came up to the machine and shook hands with Miss Josephine. "I was headed directly for Hollis Creek Inn. Your brother wrote me that you were expected to arrive there yesterday evening, and I was dropping over to call on you right away this morning. I see, however, that I was not quite prompt enough. You're selfish, Mr. Turner. You knew I was going over to Hollis Creek, and you might have invited me to ride in your machine."

"You might have invited me to walk with you," retorted Sam.

"But you knew that I was coming and I didn't know that you even knew—" he paused abruptly and fixed a contemplative eye upon young Mr. Turner, who was now surveying the scenery and Mr. Princeman in calm enjoyment.

The arrival at this moment of a cloud of dust out of which evolved a lone horseman, and that horseman Billy Westlake, added a new angle to the situation, and for one fleeting moment the three men eyed one another in mutual sheepish guilt.

"Rather good sport, I call it, Miss Stevens," declared Billy, aware of a sudden increase in his estimation of Mr. Turner, and letting the cat completely out of the bag. "Each of us was trying to steal a march on the rest, but Mr. Turner used the most businesslike method, and of course he won the race."

"I'm flattered, I'm sure," said Miss Josephine demurely. "I really feel that I ought to go right back to the house and be the belle of the ball; but it's impossible for an hour or so in this case," and she turned to her escort with the smile of mischief which she had worn the first time he saw her. "You see, we are out on a little business trip, Mr. Turner and myself. We're going to buy a walnut grove."

Mr. Turner turned upon her a glance which was half a frown.

"I promised to get you back in two hours, and I'll do it," he stated, "but we mustn't linger much by the wayside."

"With which hint we shall wend our Hollis Creek-ward way," laughed Princeman, exchanging a glance of amusement with Miss Stevens. "I think we shall visit with your father until you come back."

"Please do," she urged. "He will be as glad to see you both as I am," with which information she settled herself back in her seat with a little air of the interview being over, and the chauffeur, with proper intuition, started the machine, while Mr. Princeman and Billy looked after them glumly.

"Queer chap, isn't he?" commented Billy.

"Queer? Well, hardly that," returned Princeman thoughtfully. "There's one thing certain; he's enterprising and vigorous enough to command respect, in business or—anything else."

At about that very moment Mr. Turner was impressing upon his companion a very important bit of ethics.

"You shouldn't have violated my confidence," he told her severely.

"How was that?" she asked in surprise, and with a trifle of indignation as well.

"You told them that we were going to buy a walnut grove. You ought never to let slip anything you happen to know of any man's business plans."

"Oh!" she said blankly.

Having voiced his straightforward objection, and delivered his simple but direct lesson, Mr. Turner turned as decisively to other matters.

"Son," he asked, leaning over toward the chauffeur, "are there any speed limit laws on these roads?"

"None that I know of," replied the boy.

"Then cut her loose. Do you object to fast driving, Miss Stevens?"

"Not at all," she told him, either much chastened by the late rebuke or much amused by it. She could scarcely tell which, as yet. "I don't particularly long for a broken neck, but I never can feel that my time has come."

"It hasn't," returned Sam. "Let's see your palm," and taking her hand he held it up before him. It was a small hand that he saw, and most gracefully formed, but a strong one, too, and Sam Turner had an extremely quick and critical eye for both strength and beauty. "You are going to live to be a gray-haired grandmother," he announced after an inspection of her pink palm, "and live happily all your life."

It was noteworthy that no matter what his impulse may have been he did not hold her hand overly long, nor subject it to undue warmth of pressure, but restored it gently to her lap. She was remarking upon this herself as she took that same hand and passed its tapering fingers deftly among the twigs of the tree-bouquet, arranging a leaf here and a berry there.

CHAPTER IV.
A LITTLE VACATION PASTIME IN
WHICH GREEK MEETS GREEK

Old man Gifford was not at home in his squat, low-roofed farm-house, but a woman shaped like a pyramid of diminishing pumpkins directed them down through the grove to the corn patch. It was necessary to lift strenuously upon the sagging end of a squeaky old gate, and scrape it across gulleys, to get the automobile into the narrow, deeply-rutted road, and with a mind fearful of tires the chauffeur wheeled down through the grove quite slowly, a slowness for which Sam was duly grateful, since it allowed him to take a careful appraisement of the walnut trees, interspersed with occasional oaks, which bordered both sides of their path. They were tall, thick, straight-trunked trees, from amongst which the underbrush had been carefully cut away. It was a joy to his now vandal soul, this grove, and already he could see those majestic trunks, after having been sawed with as little wasteful chopping as possible, toppling in endless billowy furrows.

Old man Gifford came inquiringly up between the long rows of corn to the far edge of the grove. He was bent and weazened, and more gnarled than any of his trees, and even his fingers seemed to have the knotty, angular effect of twigs. A fringe of gray beard surrounded his clean-shaven face, which was criss-crossed with innumerable little furrows that the wind and rain had worn in it; but a pair of shrewd old eyes twinkled from under his bushy eyebrows.

"Morning, 'Ennery," he said, addressing the chauffeur with a squeaky little voice in which, though after forty years of residence in America, there was still a strong trace of British accent; and then his calculating gaze rested calmly in turns upon the other occupants of the machine.

"Good morning, Mr. Gifford," returned the chauffeur. "Fine day, isn't it?"

"Good corn-ripenin' weather," agreed the old man, squinting at the sky from force of habit, and then, being satisfied that there was no threatening cloud in all the visible blue expanse, he returned to a calm consideration of the strangers, waiting patiently for Mr. Turner to introduce himself.

"I understand, Mr. Gifford, that you are open to an offer for your walnut trees," began Mr. Turner, looking at his watch.

"Well, I might be," admitted the old man cautiously.

"I see," returned Sam; "that is, you might be interested if the price were right. Let's get right down to brass tacks. How much do you want?"

"Standin' or cut?"

"Well, say standing?"

"How much do you offer?"

Miss Stevens' gaze roved from the one to the other and found enjoyment in the fact that here Greek had met Greek.

Sam's reply was prompt and to the point. He named a price.

"No," said the old man instantly. "I been a-holdin' out for five dollars a thousand more than that."

Things were progressing. A basis for haggling had been established. Sam Turner, however, had the advantage. He knew the sharp advance in walnut announced that morning. Old man Gifford would not be aware of it until the rural free delivery brought his evening paper, of the night before, some time that afternoon. In view of the recent advance, even at Mr. Gifford's price there was a handsome profit in the transaction.

"The reason you've had to hold out for your rate until right now was that nobody would pay it," said Sam confidently. "Now I'm here to talk spot cash. I'll give you, say, a thousand dollars down, and the balance immediately upon measurement as the logs are loaded upon the cars."

The old man nodded in approval.

"The terms is all right," he said.

"How much will you take F. O. B. Restview?"

"Well, cuttin' and trimmin' and haulin' ain't much in my line," returned the old man, again cautious; "but after all, I reckon that there'd be less damage to my property if I looked after it myself. Of course, I'd have to have a profit for handlin' it. I'd feel like holdin' out for—for—" and after some hesitation he again named a figure.

"You've made that same proposition to others," charged Sam shrewdly, "and you couldn't get the price." Upon the heels of this he made his own offer.

The old man shook his head and turned as if to start back to the corn field.

"No, I can get better than that," he declared, shaking his head.

"Come back here and let's talk turkey," protested Sam compellingly. "You name the very lowest price you'll take, delivered on board the cars at Restview."

The old man reached down, pulled up a blade of grass, chewed it carefully, spit it out, and named his very, very lowest price; then he added: "What's the most you'll give?"

Miss Stevens leaned forward intently.

Sam very promptly named a figure five dollars lower.

"I'll split the difference with you," offered the old man.

"It's a bargain!" said Sam, and reaching into the inside pocket of his tennis coat, he brought out some queer furniture for that sort of garment—a small fountain pen and an extremely small card-case, from the latter of which he drew four folded blank checks.

He reached over and borrowed the chauffeur's enameled cap, dusted it carefully with his handkerchief, laid a check upon it and held his fountain pen poised. "What are your initials, please, Mr. Gifford?"

"Wait a minute," said the old man hastily. "Don't make out that check just yet. I don't do any business or sign any contracts till I talk with Hepseba."

"All right. Climb right in with Henry there," directed Sam, seizing upon the chauffeur's name. "We'll drive straight up to see her."

"I'll walk," firmly declared Mr. Gifford. "I never have rode in one of them things, and I'm too old to begin."

"Very well," said Sam cheerfully, jumping out of the machine with great promptness. "I'll walk with you. Back to the house, Henry," and he started anxiously to trudge up the road with Mr. Gifford, leaving Henry to manoeuver painfully in the narrow space. After a few steps, however, a sudden thought made him turn back. "Maybe you'd rather walk up, too," he suggested to Miss Stevens.

"No, I think I'll ride," she said coldly.

He opened the door in extreme haste.

"Do come on and walk," he pleaded. "Don't hold it against me because I just don't seem to be able to think of more than one thing at a time; but I was so wrapped up in this deal that— Really," and he sank his voice confidentially, "I have a tremendous bargain here, and I'll be nervous about it until I have it clenched. I'll tell you why as we go home."

He held out his hand as a matter of course to help her down. The white of his eyes was remarkably clear, the irises were remarkably blue, the pupils remarkably deep. Suddenly her face cleared and she laughed.

"It was silly of me to be snippy, wasn't it?" she confessed, as she took his hand and stepped lightly to the ground. It had just recurred to her that when he knew Princeman was walking over to see her he had said nothing, but had engaged an automobile.

Old man Gifford had nothing much to say when they caught up with him. Mr. Turner tried him with remarks about the weather, and received full information, but when he attempted to discuss the details of the walnut purchase, he received but mere grunts in reply, except finally this:

"There's no use, young man. I won't talk about them trees till I get Hepseba's opinion."

At the house Hepseba waddled out on the little stoop in response to old man Gifford's call, and stood regarding the strangers stonily through her narrow little slits of eyes.

"This gentleman, Hepseba," said old man Gifford, "wants to buy my walnut trees. What do you think of him?"

In response to that leading question, Hepseba studied Sam Turner from head to foot with the sort of scrutiny under which one slightly reddens.

"I like him," finally announced Hepseba, in a surprisingly liquid and feminine voice. "I like both of them," an unexpected turn which brought a flush to the face of Miss Stevens.

"All right, young man," said old man Gifford briskly. "Now, then, you come in the front room and write your contract, and I'll take your check."

All alacrity and open cordiality now, he led the way into the queer-old front room, musty with the solemnity of many dim Sundays.

"Just set down here in this easy chair, Mrs.— What did you say your name is?" Mr. Gifford inquired, turning to Sam.

"Turner; Sam J. Turner," returned that gentleman, grinning. "But this is Miss Stevens."

"No offense meant or taken, I hope," hastily said the old man by way of apology; "but I do say that Mr. Turner would be lucky if he had such a pretty wife."

"You have both good taste and good judgment, Mr. Gifford," commented Sam as airily as he could; then he looked across at Miss Stevens and laughed aloud, so openly and so ingenuously that, so far from the laughter giving offense, it seemed, strangely enough, to put Miss Josephine at her ease, though she still blushed furiously. There was nothing in that laugh nor in his look but frank, boyish enjoyment of the joke.

There ensued a crisp and decisive conversation between Mr. Gifford and Mr. Turner about the details of their contract, and 'Ennery was presently called in to append to it his painfully precise signature in vertical writing, Miss Stevens adding hers in a pretty round hand. Then Hepseba, to bind the bargain, brought in hot apple pie fresh from the oven, and they became quite a little family party indeed, and very friendly, 'Ennery sitting in the parlor with them and eating his pie with a fork.

"I know what Hepseba thinks," said old man Gifford, as he held the door of the car open for them. "She thinks you're a mighty keen young man that has to be watched in the beginning of a bargain, because you'll give as little as you can; but that after the bargain's made you don't need any more watching. But Lord love you, I have to be watched in a bargain myself. I take everything I can."

As he finished saying this he was closing the door of the car, but Hepseba called to them to wait, and came puffing out of the house with a little bundle wrapped in a newspaper.

"I brought this out for your wife," she said to Mr. Turner, and handed it to Miss Josephine. "It's some geranium slips. Everybody says I got the very finest geraniums in the bottoms here."

"Goodness, Hepseba," exclaimed old man Gifford, highly delighted; "that ain't his wife. That's Miss Stevens. I made the same mistake," and he hawhawed in keen enjoyment.

Hepseba was so evidently overcome with mortification, however, and her huge round face turned so painfully red, that Miss Stevens lost entirely any embarrassment she might otherwise have felt.

"It doesn't matter at all, I assure you, Mrs. Gifford," she said with charming eagerness to set Hepseba at ease. "I am very fond of geraniums, and I shall plant these slips and take good care of them. I thank you very, very much for them."

As the machine rolled away Hepseba turned to old man Gifford:

"I like both of them!" she stated most decisively.

CHAPTER V.
MISS JOSEPHINE'S FATHER AGREES THAT SAM TURNER IS ALL BUSINESS

"And now," announced Sam in calm triumph as they neared Hollis Creek Inn, "I'll finish up this deal right away. There is no use in my holding for a further rise at this time, and I'll just sell these trees to your father."

"To father!" she gasped, and then, as it dawned upon her that she had been out all morning to help Sam Turner buy up trees to sell to her own father at a profit, she burst forth into shrieks of laughter.

"What's the joke?" Sam asked, regarding her in amazement, and then, more or less dimly, he perceived. "Still," he said, relapsing into serious consideration of the affair, "your father will be in luck to buy those trees at all, even at the ten dollars a thousand profit he'll have to pay me. There is not less than a hundred thousand feet of walnut in that grove."

"Mercy!" she said. "Why, that will make you a thousand dollars for this morning's drive; and the opportunity was entirely accidental, one which would not have occurred if you hadn't come over to see me in this machine. I think I ought to have a commission."

"You ought to be fined," Sam retorted. "You had me scared stiff at one time."

"How was that?" she demanded.

"Why, of course you didn't think, but when you told the boys that I was going out to buy a walnut grove, they were right on their way to see your father. It would have been very natural for one of them to mention our errand. Your father might have immediately inquired where there was walnut to be found, and have telephoned to old man Gifford before I could reach him."

"You needn't have worried!" stated Miss Josephine in a tone so indignant that Sam turned to her in astonishment. "My father would not have done anything so despicable as that, I am quite sure!"

"He wouldn't!" exclaimed Sam. "I'll bet he would. Why, how do you suppose your father became rich in the lumber trade if it wasn't through snapping up bargains every time he found one?"

"I have no doubt that my father has been and is a very alert business man," retorted Miss Josephine most icily; "but after he knew that you had started out actually to purchase a tract of lumber, he would certainly consider that you had established a prior claim upon the property."

"Your father's name is Theophilus Stevens, isn't it?"

"Yes."

"Humph!" said Sam, but he did not explain that exclamation, nor was he asked to explain. Miss Stevens had been deeply wounded by the assault upon her father's business morality, and she desired to hear no further elaboration of the insult.

She was glad that they were drawing up now to the porch, glad this ride, with its many disagreeable features, was over, although she carefully gathered up her bright-berried branches, which were not half so much withered as she had expected them to be, and held her geranium slips cautiously as she alighted.

Her father came out to the edge of the porch to meet them. He paid no attention to his daughter.

"Well, Sam Turner," said Mr. Stevens, stroking his aggressive beard, "I hear you got it, confound you! What do you want for your lumber contract?"

"Just the advance of this morning's quotations," replied Sam. "Princeman tell you I was after it?"

"No, not at first," said Stevens. "I received a telegram about that grove just an hour ago, from my partner. Princeman was with me when the telegram came, and he told me then that you had just gone out on the trail. I did my best to get Gifford by 'phone before you could reach him."

"Father!" exclaimed Miss Josephine.

"What's the matter, Jo?"

"You say you actually tried to—to get in ahead of Mr. Turner in buying this lumber, knowing that he was going down there purposely for it?"

"Why, certainly," admitted her father.

"But did you know that I was with Mr. Turner?"

"Why, certainly!"

"Father!" was all she could gasp, and without deigning to say good-by to Mr. Turner, or to thank him for the ride or the bouquet of branches or even the geranium slips which she had received under false pretenses, she hurried away to her room, oppressed with Heaven only knows what mortification, and also with what wonder at the ways of men!

However, Princeman and Billy Westlake and young Hollis with the curly hair were impatiently waiting for Miss Josephine at the tennis court, as they informed her in a jointly signed note sent up to her by a boy, and hastily removing the dust of the road she ran down to join them. As she went across the lawn, tennis bat in hand, Sam Turner, discussing lumber with Mr. Stevens, saw her and stopped talking abruptly to admire the trim, graceful figure.

"Does your daughter play tennis much?" he inquired.

"A great deal," returned Mr. Stevens, expanding with pride. "Jo's a very expert player. She's better at it than any of these girls, and she really doesn't care to play except with experts. Princeman, Hollis and Billy Westlake are easily the champions here."

"I see," said Sam thoughtfully.

"I suppose you're a crack player yourself," his host resumed, glancing at Sam's bat.

"Me? No, worse than a dub. I never had time; that is, until now. I'll tell you, though, this being away from the business grind is a great thing. You don't know how I enjoy the fresh air and the being out in the country this way, and the absolute freedom from business cares and worries."

"But where are you going?" asked Stevens, for Sam was getting up. "You'll stay to lunch with us, won't you?"

"No, thanks," replied Sam, looking at his watch. "I expect some word from my kid brother. I have wired him to send some samples of marsh pulp, and the paper we've had made from it."

"Marsh pulp," repeated Mr. Stevens. "That's a new one on me. What's it like?"

"Greatest stunt on earth," replied Sam confidently. "It is our scheme to meet the deforestation danger on the way—coming."

Already he was reaching in his pocket for paper and pencil, and sat down again at the side of Mr. Stevens, who immediately began stroking his aggressive beard. Fifteen minutes later Sam briskly got up again and Mr. Stevens shook hands with him.

"That's a great scheme," he said, and he gazed after Sam's broad shoulders admiringly as that young man strode down the steps.

On his way Sam passed the tennis court where the one girl and three young men were engaged in a most dextrous game, a game which all the other amateurs of Hollis Creek Inn had stopped their own sets to watch. In the pause of changing sides Miss Josephine saw him and waved her hand and wafted a gay word to him. A second later she was in the air, a lithe, graceful figure, meeting a high "serve," and Sam walked on quite thoughtfully.

When he arrived at Meadow Brook his first care was for his telegram. It was there, and bore the assurance that the samples would arrive on the following morning. His next step was to hunt Miss Westlake. That plump young person forgot her pique of the morning in an instant when he came up to her with that smiling "been-looking-for-you-everywhere, mighty-glad-to-see-you" cordiality.

"I want you to teach me tennis," he said immediately.

"I'm afraid I can't teach you much," she replied with becoming diffidence, "because I'm not a good enough player myself; but I'll do my best. We'll have a set right after luncheon; shall we?"

"Fine!" said he.

After luncheon Mr. Westlake and Mr. Cuthbert waylaid him, but he merely thrust his telegram into Mr. Westlake's hands, and hurried off to the tennis grounds with Miss Westlake and Miss Hastings and lanky Bob Tilloughby, who stuttered horribly and blushed when he spoke, and was in deadly seriousness about everything. Never did a man work so hard at anything as Sam Turner worked at tennis. He had a keen eye and a dextrous wrist, and he kept the game up to top-notch speed. Of course he made blunders and became confused in his count and overlooked opportunities, but he covered acres of ground, as Vivian Hastings expressed it, and when, at the end of an hour, they sat down, panting, to rest, young Tilloughby, with painful earnestness, assured him that he had "the mum-mum-makings of a fine tennis player."

Sam considered that compliment very thoughtfully, but he was a trifle dubious. Already he perceived that tennis playing was not only an occupation but a calling.

"Thanks," said he. "It's mighty nice of you to say so, Tilloughby. What's the next game?"

"The nun-nun-next game is a stroll," Tilloughby soberly advised him. "It always stus-stus-starts out as a foursome, and ends up in tut-tut-two doubles."

So they strolled. They wound along the brookside among some of the pretty paths, and in the rugged places Miss Westlake threw her weight upon Sam's helping arm as much as possible; in the concealed places she languished, which she did very prettily, she thought, considering her one hundred and sixty-three pounds. They took him through a detour of shady paths which occupied a full hour to traverse, but this particular game did not wind up in "two doubles." In spite of all the excellent tête-à-tête opportunities which should have risen for both couples, Miss Westlake was annoyed to find Miss Hastings right close behind, and holding even the conversation to a foursome.

In the meantime, Sam Turner took careful lessons in the art of talking twaddle, and they never knew that he was bored. Having entered into the game he played it with spirit, and before they had returned to the house Mr. Tilloughby was calling him Sus-Sus-Sam.

The girls disappeared for their beauty sleep, and Sam found McComas and Billy Westlake hunting for him.

"Do you play base-ball?" inquired McComas.

"A little. I used to catch, to help out my kid brother, who is an expert pitcher."

"Good!" said McComas, writing down Sam's name. "Princeman will pitch, but we needed a catcher. The rivalry between Meadow Brook and Hollis Creek is intense this year. They've captured nearly all the early trophies, but we're going over there next week for a match game and we're about crazy to win."

"I'll do the best I can," promised Sam. "Got a base-ball? We'll go out and practise."

They slammed hot ones into each other for a half hour, and when they had enough of it, McComas, wiping his brow, exclaimed approvingly:

"You'll do great with a little more warming up. We have a couple of corking players, but we need them. Hollis always pitches for Hollis Creek, and he usually wins his game. On baseball day he's the idol of all the girls."

Sam Turner placed his hand meditatively upon the back of his neck as he walked in to dress for dinner. Making a good impression upon the girls was a separate business, it seemed, and one which required much preparation. Well, he was in for the entire circus, but he realized that he was a little late in starting. In consequence he could not afford to overlook any of the points; so, before dressing for dinner, he paid a quiet visit to the greenhouses.

That evening, while he was bowling with all the earnestness that in him lay, Josephine Stevens, resisting the importunities of young Hollis for some music, sat by her father.

"Father," she asked after long and sober thought, "was it right for you, knowing Mr. Turner to be after that walnut lumber, to try to get it away from him by telephoning?"

"It certainly was!" he replied emphatically. "Turner went down there with a deliberate intention of buying that lumber before I could get it, so that he could sell it to me at as big a gain as possible. I paid him one thousand dollars profit for his contract. I had struggled my best to beat him to it; only I was too late. Both of us were playing the game according to the rules, but he is a younger player."

"I see." Another long pause. "Here's another thing. Mr. Turner happened to know of this increase in the price of lumber, and he hurried down there to a man who didn't know about that, and bought it. If Mr. Gifford had known of the new rates, Mr. Turner could not have bought those trees at the price he did, could he?"

"Certainly not," agreed her father. "He would have had to pay nearly a thousand dollars more for them."

"Then that wasn't right of Mr. Turner," she asserted.

"My child," said Mr. Stevens wearily, "all business is conducted for a profit, and the only way to get it is by keeping alive and knowing things that other people will find out to-morrow. Sam Turner is the shrewdest and the livest young man I've met in many a day, and he's square as a die. I'd take his word on any proposition; wouldn't you?"

"Yes, I think I'd take his word," she admitted, and very positively, after mature deliberation. "But truly, father, don't you think he's too much concentrated on business? He hasn't a thought in his mind for anything else. For instance, this morning he came over to take me an automobile ride around Bald Hill, and when he found out about this walnut grove, without either apology or explanation to me he ordered the chauffeur to drive right down there."

"Fine," laughed her father. "I'd like to hire him for my manager, if I could only offer him enough money. But I don't see your point of criticism. It seems to me that he's a mighty presentable and likable young fellow, good looking, and a gentleman in the sense in which I like to use that word."

"Yes, he is all of those things," she admitted again; "but it is a flaw in a young man, isn't it," she persisted, betraying an unusually anxious interest, "for him never to think of a solitary thing but just business?"

They were sitting in one of the alcoves of the assembly room, and at that moment a bell-boy, wandering around the place with apparent aimlessness, spied them and brought to Miss Josephine a big box. She opened it and an exclamation of pleasure escaped her. In the box was a huge bouquet of exquisite roses, soft and glowing, delicious in their fragrance.

Impulsively she buried her face in them.

"Oh, how delightful!" she cried, and she drew out the white card which peeped forth from amidst the stems. "They are from Mr. Turner!" she gasped.

"You're quite right about him," commented her father dryly. "He's all business."

CHAPTER VI.
IN WHICH THE SUMMER LOAFER ORDERS
SOME MARASCHINO CHOCOLATES

Before Sam had his breakfast the next morning, he sat in his room with some figures with which Blackrock and Cuthbert had provided him the evening before. He cast them up and down and crosswise and diagonally, balanced them and juggled them and sorted them and shifted them, until at last he found the rat hole, and smiling grimly, placed those pages of neat figures in a small letter file which he took from his trunk. One thing was certain: the Meadow Brook capitalists were highly interested in his plan, or they would never go to the trouble to devise, so early in the game, a scheme for gaining control of the marsh pulp corporation. Well, they were the exact people he wanted.

Immediately after breakfast Miss Stevens telephoned over to thank him for his beautiful roses, and he had the pleasure of letting her know, quite incidentally, that he had gone down to the rose-beds and picked out each individual blossom himself, which, of course, accounted for their excellence. Also he suggested coming over that morning for a brief walk.

No, she was very sorry, but she was just making ready to go out horseback riding with Mr. Hollis, who, by the way, was an excellent rider; but they would be back from their canter about ten-thirty, and if Mr. Turner cared to come over for a game of tennis before luncheon, why—

"Sorry I can't do it," returned Mr. Turner with the deepest of genuine regret in his tone. "My kid brother is sending me some samples of pulp and paper which will arrive at about eleven o'clock, and I have called a meeting of some interested parties here to examine them at about eleven."

"Business again," she protested. "I thought you were on a vacation."

"I am," he assured her in surprise. "I never lazied around so or frittered up so much time in my life; and I'm enjoying every second of my freedom, too. I tell you, it's fine. But say, this meeting won't take over an hour. Why can't I come over right after lunch?"

She was very sorry, this time a little less regretfully, that after luncheon she had an engagement with Mr. Princeman to play a match game of croquet. But, and here she relented a trifle, they were getting up a hasty, informal dance over at Hollis Creek for that evening. Would he come over?

He certainly would, and he already spoke for as many dances as she would give him.

"I'll give you what I can," she told him; "but I've already promised three of them to Billy Westlake, who is a divine dancer."

Sam Turner was deeply thoughtful as he turned away from the telephone. Hollis was a superb horseback rider. Billy Westlake was a divine dancer. Princeman, he had learned from Miss Stevens, who had spoken with vast enthusiasm, was a base-ball hero. Hollis and Princeman and Westlake were crack bowlers, also crack tennis players, and no doubt all three were even expert croquet players. It was easy to see the sort of men she admired. Sam Turner only knew one recipe to get things, and he had made up his mind to have Miss Stevens. He promptly sought Miss Westlake.

"Do you ride?" he wanted to know.

"Not as often as I'd like," she said.

Really, she had half promised to go driving with Tilloughby, but it was not an actual promise, and if it were she was quite willing to get out of it, if Mr. Turner wanted her to go along, although she did not say so. Young Tilloughby was notoriously an impossible match. But possibly Mr. Tilloughby and Miss Hastings might care to join the party. She suggested it.

"Why, certainly," said Sam heartily. "The more the merrier," which was not the thing she wanted him to say.

Tilloughby, a trifle disappointed yet very gracious, consented to ride in place of drive, and Miss Hastings was only too delighted; entirely too much so, Miss Westlake thought. Accordingly they rode, and Sam insisted on lagging behind with Miss Westlake, which she took to be of considerable significance, and exhibited a very obvious fluttering about it. Sam's motive, however, was to watch Tilloughby in the saddle, for in their conversation it had developed that Tilloughby was a very fair rider; and everything that he saw Tilloughby do, Sam did. En route they met Hollis and Miss Stevens, cantering just where the Bald Hill road branched off, and the cavalcade was increased to six. Once, in taking a narrow cross-cut down through the woods, Sam had the felicity of riding beside Miss Stevens for a moment, and she put her hand on his horse and patted its glossy neck and admired it, while Sam admired the hand. He felt, in some way or other, that riding for that ten yards by her side was a sort of triumph over Hollis, until he saw her dash up presently by the side of Hollis again and chat brightly with that young gentleman.

Thereafter Sam quit watching Tilloughby and watched Hollis. Curly-head was an accomplished rider, and Sam felt that he himself cut but an awkward figure. In reality he was too conscious of his defects. By strict attention he was proving himself a fair ordinary rider, but when Hollis, out of sheer showiness, turned aside from the path to jump his horse over a fallen tree, and Miss Stevens out of bravado followed him, Sam Turner well-nigh ground his teeth, and, acting upon the impulse, he too attempted the jump. The horse got over safely, but Sam went a cropper over his head, and not being a particle hurt had to endure the good-natured laughter of the balance of them. Miss Stevens seemed as much amused as any one! He had not caught her look of fright as he fell nor of concern as he rose, nor could he estimate that her laugh was a mild form of hysteria, encouraged because it would deceive. What an ass he was, he savagely thought, to exhibit himself before her in an attempt like that, without sufficient preparation! He must ride every morning, by himself.

Miss Josephine and Mr. Hollis were bound for the Bald Hill circle, and they insisted, the insistence being largely on the part of Miss Stevens, on the others accompanying them; but Mr. Turner's engagement at eleven o'clock would not admit of this, and reluctantly he took Miss Hastings back with him, leaving Miss Westlake and young Tilloughby to go on. The arrangement suited him very well, for at least Hollis' ride with Miss Stevens would not be a tête-à-tête. Miss Westlake strove to let him understand as plainly as she could that she was only going with Mr. Tilloughby because of her previous semi-engagement with him—and there seemed a coolness between Miss Westlake and Miss Hastings as they separated. Miss Hastings did her best on the way back to console Mr. Turner for the absence of Miss Westlake. Vivacious as she always was, she never was more so than now, and before Sam knew it he had engaged himself with her to gather ferns in the afternoon.

Upon his arrival at Meadow Brook, he found his express package and also a couple of important letters awaiting him, and immediately held on the porch a full meeting of the tentative Marsh Pulp Company. In that meeting he decided on four things: first, that these hard-headed men of business were highly favorable to his scheme; second, that Princeman and Cuthbert, who knew most about paper and pulp, were so profoundly impressed with his samples that they tried to conceal it from him; third, that Princeman, at first his warmest adherent, was now most stubbornly opposed to him, not that he wished to prevent forming the company, but that he wished to prevent Sam's having his own way; fourth, that the crowd had talked it over and had firmly determined that Sam should not control their money. Princeman was especially severe.

"There is no question but that these samples are convincing of their own excellence," he admitted; "but properly to estimate the value of both pulp and paper, it would be necessary to know, by rigid experiment, the precise difficulties of manufacture, to say nothing of the manner in which these particular specimens were produced."

Mr. Princeman's words had undoubted weight, casting, as they did, a clammy suspicion upon Sam's samples.

"I had thought of that," confessed Mr. Turner, "and had I not been prepared to meet such a natural doubt, to say nothing of such a natural insinuation, I should never have submitted these samples. Mr. Princeman, do you know G. W. Creamer of the Eureka Paper Mills?"

Mr. Princeman, with a wince, did, for G. W. Creamer and the Eureka Paper Mills were his most successful competitors in the manufacture of special-priced high-grade papers. Mr. Cuthbert also knew Mr. Creamer intimately.

"Good," said Sam; "then Mr. Creamer's letter will have some weight," and he turned it over to Mr. Blackrock. That gentleman, setting his spectacles astride his nose and assuming his most profoundly professional air, read aloud the letter in which Mr. Creamer thanked Turner and Turner for reposing confidence enough in him to reveal their process and permit him to make experiments, and stated, with many convincing facts and figures, that he had made several separate samples of the pulp in his experimental shop, and from the pulp had made paper, samples of which he enclosed under separate cover, stating further that the pulp could be manufactured far cheaper than wood pulp, and that the quality of the paper, in his estimation, was even superior; and when the company was formed, he wished to be set down for a good, fat block of stock.

Having submitted exhibit A in the form of his brother's samples of pulp and paper, exhibit B in the form of Mr. Creamer's letter, and exhibit C in the form of Mr. Creamer's own samples of pulp and paper, Mr. Turner rested quite comfortably in his chair, thank you.

"This seems to make the thing positive," admitted Mr. Princeman. "Mr. Turner, would you mind sending some samples of your material to my factory with the necessary instructions?"

"Not at all," replied Sam suavely. "We would be pleased indeed to do so, just as soon as our patents are allowed."

"Pending that," suggested Mr. Westlake placidly, looking out over the brook, "why couldn't we organize a sort of tentative company? Why couldn't we at least canvass ourselves and see how much of Mr. Turner's stock we would take up among us?"

"That is," put in Mr. Cuthbert, screwing the remark out of himself sidewise, "provided the terms of incorporation and promotion were satisfactory to us."

"I have already drawn up a sort of preliminary proposition, after consultation with our friends here," Mr. Blackrock now stated, "and purely as a tentative matter it might be read."

"Go right ahead," directed Sam. "I'm a good listener."

Mr. Blackrock slowly and ponderously read the proposed plan of incorporation. Sam rose and looked at his watch.

"It won't do," he announced sharply. "That whole thing, in accordance with the figures you submitted me last night, is framed up for the sole purpose of preventing my ever securing control, and if I do not have a chance, at least, at control, I won't play."

"You seem to be very sure of that," said Mr. Princeman, surveying him coldly; "but there is another thing equally sure, and that is that you can not engage capital in as big an enterprise as this on any basis which will separate the control and the money."

"I'm going to try it, though," retorted Sam. "If I can't separate the control and the money I suppose I'll have to put up with the best terms I can get. If you will let me have that prospectus of yours, Mr. Blackrock, I'll take it up to my room and study it, and draw up a counter prospectus of my own."

"With pleasure," said Mr. Blackrock, handing it over courteously, and Mr. Turner rose.

"I'll say this much, Sam," stated Mr. Westlake, who seemed to have grown more friendly as Mr. Princeman grew cooler; "if you can get a proposition upon which we are all agreed, I'll take fifty thousand of that stock myself, at fifty."

"As a matter of fact, Mr. Turner," added Mr. Cuthbert, "including your friend Creamer, who insists upon being in, I imagine that we can finance your entire company right in this crowd—if the terms are right."

"Nothing would give me greater pleasure, I'm sure," said Mr. Turner, and bowed himself away.

In place of going to his room, however, he went to the telegraph office, and wired his brother in New York:

"How are you coming on with pulp company stock subscription?"

The telegraph office was in one corner of the post-office, which was also a souvenir room, with candy and cigar counters, and as he turned away from the telegraph desk he saw Princeman at the candy counter.

"No, I don't care for any of these," Princeman was saying. "If you haven't maraschino chocolates I don't want any."

Sam immediately stepped back to the telegraph desk and sent another wire to his brother:

"Express fresh box maraschino chocolates to Miss Josephine Stevens Hollis Creek Inn enclose my card personal cards in upper right-hand pigeonhole my desk."

Then he went up-stairs to get ready for lunch. Immediately after luncheon he received the following wire from his brother:

"Stock subscription rotten everybody likes scheme but object to our control but no hurry why don't you rest maraschinos shipped congratulate you."

CHAPTER VII.
WHICH EXHIBITS THE IMPORTANCE
OF REMEMBERING A DANCE NUMBER

And so the kid was finding the same trouble which he had met. They had been too frank in stating that they intended to obtain control of the company without any larger investments than their patents and their scheme. Sam wandered through the hall, revolving this matter in his mind, and out at the rear door, which framed an inviting vista of green. He strolled back past the barn toward the upper reaches of the brook path, and sitting amid the comfortably gnarled roots of a big tree he lit a cigar and began with violence to snap little pebbles into the brook. If he were promoting a crooked scheme, he reflected savagely, he would have no difficulty whatever in floating it upon almost any terms he wanted. Well, there was one thing certain; at the finish, control would be in his own hands! But how to secure it and still float the company promptly and advantageously? There was the problem. He liked this crowd. They were good, keen, vigorous, enterprising men, fine men with whom to do business, men who would snatch control away from him if they could, and throw him out in the cold in a minute if they deemed it necessary or expedient. Of course that was to be expected. It was a part of the game. He would rather deal with these progressive people, knowing their tendencies, than with a lot of sapheads.

How to get control? He lingered long and thoughtfully over that question, perhaps an hour, until presently he became aware that a slight young girl, with a fetching sun-hat and a basket, was walking pensively along the path on the opposite side of the brook, for the third time. Her passing and repassing before his abstracted and unseeing vision had become slightly monotonous, and for the first time he focused his eyes back from their distant view of pulp marshes and stock certificates and inspected the girl directly. Why, he knew that girl! It was Miss Hastings.

As if in obedience to his steady gaze she looked across at him and waved her basket.

"Where are you going?" he asked with the heartiness of enforced courtesy.

"After ferns," she responded, and laughed.

"By George, that's so!" he said, and ran up the stream to a narrow place where he made a magnificent jump and only got one shoe wet.

He was profuse, not in his apologies, but in his intention to make them.

"Jinks!" he said. "I'm ashamed to say I forgot all about that. I found myself suddenly confronted with a business proposition that had to be worked out, and I thought of nothing else."

"I hope you succeeded," she said pleasantly.

There wasn't a particle of vengefulness about Miss Hastings. She was not one to hold this against him; he could see that at once! She understood men. She knew that grave problems frequently confronted them, and that such minor things as fern gathering expeditions would necessarily have to step aside and be forgotten. She was one of the bright, cheerful, always smiling kind; one who would make a sunshiny helpmate for any man, and never object to anything he did—before marriage.

All this she conveyed in lively but appealing chatter; all, that is, except the last part of it, a deduction which Sam supplied for himself. For the first time in his life he had paused to judge a girl as he would "size up" a man, and he was a little bit sorry that he had done so, for while Miss Hastings was very agreeable, there was a certain acidulous sharpness about her nose and uncompromising thinness about her lips which no amount of laughing vivacity could quite conceal.

Dutifully, however, he gathered ferns for the rockery of her aunt in Albany, and Miss Hastings, in return, did her best to amuse and delight, and delicately to convey the thought of what an agreeable thing it would be for a man always to have this cheerful companionship. She even, on the way back, went so far as inadvertently to call him Sam, and apologized immediately in the most charming confusion.

"Really," she added in explanation, "I have heard Mr. Westlake and the others call you Sam so often that the name just seems to slip out."

"That's right," he said cordially. "Sam's my name. When people call me Mr. Turner I know they are strangers."

"Then I think I shall call you Sam," she said, laughing most engagingly. "It's so much easier," and sure enough she did as soon as they were well within the hearing of Miss Westlake, at the hotel.

"Oh, Sam," she called, turning in the doorway, "you have my gloves in your pocket."

Miss Westlake stiffened like an icicle, and a stern resolve came upon her. Whatever happened, she saw her duty plainly before her. She had introduced Mr. Turner to Miss Hastings, and she was responsible. It was her moral obligation to rescue him from the clutches of that designing young person, and she immediately reminded him that she had an engagement to give him a tennis lesson every day. There was still time for a set before dinner. Also, far be it from her to be so forward as to call him Sam, or to annoy him with silly chattering. She was serious-minded, was Miss Westlake, and sweet and helpful; any man could see that; and she fairly adored business. It was so interesting.

When they came back from their tennis game, hurrying because it was high time to dress for dinner and the dance, she met Miss Hastings in the hall, but the two bosom friends barely nodded. There had sprung up an unaccountable coolness between them, a coolness which Sam by no means noticed, however, for at the far end of the porch sat Princeman, already back from Hollis Creek to dress, and with him were Westlake and McComas and Blackrock and Cuthbert, and they were in very close conference. When Sam approached them they stopped talking abruptly for just one little moment, then resumed the conversation quite naturally, even more than quite naturally in fact, and the experienced Sam smiled grimly as he excused himself to dress.

Billy Westlake met him as he was going up-stairs. To Billy had been entrusted the office of rounding up all the young people who were going over to Hollis Creek, and by previous instruction, though wondering at his sister's choice, he assigned Sam to that young lady, a fate which Sam accepted with becoming gratitude.

He had plenty of food for thought as he donned his costume of dead black and staring white, and somehow or other he was distrait that evening all the way over to Hollis Creek. Only when he met Miss Stevens did he brighten, as he might well do, for Miss Stevens, charming in every guise, was a revelation in evening costume; a ravishing revelation; one to make a man pause and wonder and stand in awe, and regard himself as a clumsy creature not worthy to touch the hem of the garment which embellished such a divine being. Nevertheless he conquered that wave of diffidence in a jiffy, or something like half that space of time, and shook hands with her most eagerly, and looked into her eyes and was grateful; for he found them smiling up at him in most friendly fashion, and with rather an electric thrill in them, too, though whether the thrill emanated from the eyes or was merely within himself he was not sure.

"How many dances do I get?" he abruptly demanded.

"Just two," she told him, and showed him her card and gave him one on which a list of names had already been marked by the young ladies of Hollis Creek.

He saw on the card two dances with Miss Stevens, one each with Miss Westlake and Miss Hastings, and one each with a number of other young ladies whom he had met but vaguely, and one each with some whom he had not met at all. He dutifully went through the first dance with a young lady of excellent connections who would make a prime companion for any advancing young man with social aspirations; he went dutifully through the next dance with a young lady who was keen on intellectual pursuits, and who would make an excellent helpmate for any young man who wished to advance in culture as he progressed in business, and danced the next one with a young lady who believed that home-making should be the highest aim of womankind; and then came his first dance with Miss Stevens! They did not talk very much, but it was very, very comforting to be with her, just to know that she was there, and to know that somehow she understood. He was sorry, though, that he stepped upon her gown.

The promenade, which had seemed quite long enough with the other young ladies, seemed all too short for Sam up to the point when Billy Westlake came to take Miss Josephine away. He was feeling rather lonely when Tilloughby came up to him, with a charming young lady who was in quite a flutter. It seemed that there had been a dreadful mistake in the making out of the dance cards, which the young ladies of Hollis Creek had endeavored to do with strict equity, though hastily, and all was now inextricable confusion. The charming young lady was on the cards for this dance with both Mr. Tilloughby and Mr. Turner, and Mr. Tilloughby had claimed her first. Would Mr. Turner kindly excuse her? Just behind her came another young lady whom Mr. Tilloughby introduced. This young lady was on Sam's card for the next dance following this one, but it should be for the eighth dance, and would Mr. Turner please change his card accordingly, which Mr. Turner obligingly did, wondering what he should do when it came to the eighth dance and he should find himself obligated to two young ladies. Oh, well, he reflected, no doubt the other young lady was down for the eighth dance with some one else, if they had things so mixed. Of one thing he was sure. He had that tenth dance with Miss Stevens. He had inspected both cards to make certain of that, and had seen with carefully concealed joy that she had compared them as minutely as he had. He saw confusion going on all about him, laughing young people attempting to straighten out the tangle, and the dance was slow in starting.

Almost the first two on the floor were Miss Stevens and Billy Westlake, and as he saw them, from his vantage point outside one of the broad windows, gliding gracefully up the far side of the room, he realized with a twinge of impatience what a remarkably unskilled dancer he himself was. Billy and Miss Stevens were talking, too, with the greatest animation, and she was looking up at Billy as brightly, even more brightly he thought, than she had at himself. There was a delicate flush on her cheeks. Her lips, full and red and deliciously curved, were parted in a smile. Confound it anyhow! What could she find to talk about with Billy Westlake?

He was turning away in more or less impatience, when Mr. Stevens, looking, in some way, with his aggressive, white, outstanding beard, as if he ought to have a red ribbon diagonally across his white shirt front, ranged beside him.

"Fine sight, isn't it?" observed Mr. Stevens.

"Yes," admitted Mr. Turner, almost shortly, and forced himself to turn away from the following of that dazzling vision, which was almost painful under the circumstances.

By mutual impulse they walked down the length of the side porch and across the front porch. Sam drew himself away from dancing and certain correlated ideas with a jerk.

"I've been wanting to talk with you, Mr. Stevens," he observed. "I think I'll drop over to-morrow for a little while."

"Glad to have you any time, Sam," responded Mr. Stevens heartily, "but there is no time like the present, you know. What's on your mind?"

"This Marsh Pulp Company," said Sam; "do you know anything about pulp and paper?"

"A little bit. You know I have some stock in Princeman's company."

"Oh," returned Sam thoughtfully.

"Not enough to hurt, however," Stevens went on. "Twenty shares, I believe. When I went in I had several times as much, but not enough to make me a dominant factor by any means, and Princeman, as he made more money, wanted some of it, so I let him buy up quite a number of shares. At one time I was very much interested, however, and visited the mills quite frequently."

"You're rather close to Princeman in a business way, aren't you?" Sam asked after duly cautious reflection.

"Not at all, although we get along very nicely indeed. I made money on my paper stock, both in dividends and in a very comfortable advance when I sold it. Our relations have always been friendly, but very little more. Why?"

"Oh, nothing. Only Princeman is much interested in my Pulp Company, and all the people who are going in are his friends. The crowd over at Meadow Brook talks of taking up approximately the entire stock of my company. I thought possibly you might be interested."

"I am right now, from what I have already heard of it," returned Stevens, who had almost at first sight succumbed to that indefinable personal appeal which caused Sam Turner to be trusted of all men. "I shall be very glad to hear more about it. It struck me when you spoke of it yesterday as a very good proposition."

They had reached the dark corner at the far end of the porch, illumined only by the subdued light which came from a half-hidden window, and now they sat down. Sam fished in the little armpit pocket of his dress coat and dragged forth two tiny samples of pulp and two tiny samples of paper.

"These two," he stated, "were samples sent me to-day by my kid brother."

Mr. Stevens took the samples and examined them with interest. He felt their texture. He twisted them and crumpled them and bent them backward and forward and tore them. Then, the light at this window being too weak, he went to one of the broad windows where a stronger stream of light came out, and examined them anew. Sam, still sitting in his chair, nodded in satisfied approval. He liked that kind of inspection. Mr. Stevens brought the samples back.

"They are excellent, so far as I am able to judge," he announced. "These are samples made by yourselves from marsh products?"

"Yes," Sam assured him. "Made from marsh-grown material by our new process, which is much cheaper than the wood-pulp process. Do you know Mr. Creamer of the Eureka Paper Mills?"

"Not very well. I've met him once or twice at dinners, but I'm not intimately acquainted with him. I hear, however, that he is an authority."

"Here's a letter from him, and some samples made by him under our process," said Sam with secret satisfaction. "I just received them this morning." From the same pocket he took the letter without its envelope, and with it handed over the two other small samples.

"That's a fine showing," Stevens commented when he had examined document and samples and brought them back, and he sat down, edging about so that he and Sam sat side by side but facing each other, as in a tête-à-tête chair. "Now tell me all about it."

On and on went the music in the ball-room, on went the shuffling of feet, the swish of garments, the gay talk and laughter of the young people; and on and on talked Mr. Stevens and Mr. Turner, until one familiar strain of music penetrated into Sam's inner consciousness; the *Home Sweet Home* waltz!

"By George!" he exclaimed, jumping up. "That can't be the last."

"Sounds like it," commented Mr. Stevens, also rising. "It is the last if they make up programs as they did in my young days. I don't remember of many dances where the *Home Sweet Home* waltz didn't end it up. It's late enough anyhow. It's eleven-thirty."

"Then I have done it again!" said Sam ruefully. "I had the number ten dance with your daughter."

Mr. Stevens closed his eyes to laugh.

"You certainly have put your foot in it," he admitted. "Oh, well, Jo's sensible," he added with a father's fond ignorance. "She'll understand."

"That's what I'm afraid of," replied Mr. Turner ruefully. "You'll have to intercede for me. Explain to her about it and soften the case as much as you can. Frankly, Mr. Stevens, I'd be tremendously cut up to be on the outs with Miss Josephine."

"There are shoals of young men who feel that way about it, Sam," said Mr. Stevens with large and commendable pride. "However, I am glad that you have added yourself to the list," and he gazed after Sam with considerable approbation, as that young man hurried away to display his abjectness to the young lady in question.

Three times, on the arm of Princeman, she whirled past the open doorway where Sam stood, but somehow or other he found it impossible to catch her eye. The dance ended when she was on the other side of the room, and immediately, with the last strains, the floor was in confusion. Sam tried desperately to hurry across to where she was, but he lost her in the crowd. He did not see her again until all of the Meadow Brook folk, including himself, were seated in the carryalls, at which time the Hollis Creek folk were at the edge of the porte-cochère and both parties were exchanging a gabbling pandemonium of good-bys. He saw her then, standing back among the crowd, and shouting her adieus as vociferously as any of them. He caught her eye and she nodded to him as pleasantly as to anybody, which was really worse than if she had refused to acknowledge him at all!

CHAPTER VIII.
NOT SAM'S FAULT THIS TIME

No, Miss Stevens was sorry that she could not go walking with him that morning, which was the morning after the dance. She was very polite about it, too; almost too polite. Her voice over the telephone was as suave and as limpid as could possibly be, but there was a sort of metallic glitter behind it, as it were.

No, she could not see him that afternoon either. She had made a series of engagements, in fact, covering the entire day. Also, she regretted to say, upon further solicitation, that she had made engagements covering the entire following day.

No, she was not piqued about his last night's forgetfulness; by no means; certainly not; how absurd!

She quite understood. He had been talking business with her father, and naturally such a trifling detail as a dance with frivolous young people would not occur to him.

Frivolous young people! This was the exact point of the conversation at which Sam, with his ear glued to the receiver of the telephone and no necessity for concealing the concerned expression on his countenance, thought, in more or less of a panic, that he must really be getting old, which was a good joke, inasmuch as nobody ever took him to be over twenty-five. Heretofore his boyish appearance had worried him because it rather stood in the way of business, but now he began to fear that he was losing it; for he was nearing thirty!

Well, pleading was of no avail. He had to give it up. Reluctantly he went out and took a solitary walk, then came in and religiously played his two hours of tennis with Miss Westlake and Miss Hastings and Tilloughby. Was he not on vacation, and must he not enjoy himself? Just before he went in to luncheon, however, there was a telephone call for him.

Miss Stevens was perplexed to know what divine intuition had told him her obsession for maraschino chocolates. She had one in her fingers at the very moment she was telephoning, and she was going to pop it into her mouth while he talked. Being a mere man he could not realize how delightfully refreshing was a maraschino chocolate.

Sam had a lively picture of that dainty confection between the tips of her dainty fingers; he could see the white hand and the graceful wrist, and then he could see those exquisitely curved red lips parting with a flash of white teeth to receive the delicacy; and he had an impulse to climb through the telephone.

A little bird had told him about her preference, he stated. He had that little bird regularly in his employ to find out other preferences.

"I had those sent just to show you that I am not altogether absorbed in business," he went on; "that I can think of other things. Have another chocolate."

"I am," she laughingly said; "but I'm not going to eat them all. I'm going to save one or two for you."

"Good," returned Sam in huge delight and relief. "I'll come over to get them any time you say."

"All right," she gaily agreed. "As I told you this morning, I have an engagement for this afternoon, but if you'll come over after luncheon I'll try to find a half-hour or so for you anyhow."

Great blotches of perspiration sprang out on his forehead.

"Jinks!" he ejaculated. "You know, right after you telephoned me this morning I made an engagement with Mr. Blackrock and Mr. Cuthbert and Mr. Westlake, to go over some proposed incorporation papers."

"Oh, by all means, then, keep your engagement," she told him, and he could feel the instant frigidity which returned to her tone. A zero-like wave seemed to come right through the transmitter of the telephone and chill the perspiration of his brow into a cold trickle.

"No, I'll see if I can not set that engagement off for a couple of hours," he hastily informed her.

"By no means," she protested, more frigidly than before. "Come to think of it, I don't believe I'd have time anyhow. In fact, I'm sure that I would not. Mr. Hollis is calling me now. Good-by."

"Wait a minute," he called desperately into the telephone, but it was dead, and there is nothing in this world so dead as the telephone from which connection has been suddenly shut off.

Sam strode into the dining-room and went straight over to Blackrock's table.

"I find I have some pressing business right after luncheon," he said, bending over that gentleman's chair. "I can't possibly meet you at two o'clock. Will four do you?"

"Why, certainly," Mr. Blackrock was kind enough to say, and he furthermore agreed, with equal graciousness, to inform the others.

Sam ate his luncheon in worried silence, replying only in monosyllables to the remarks of McComas, who sat at his table, and of Mrs. McComas, who had taken quite a young-motherly fancy to him; and the amount that he ate was so much at variance with his usual hearty appetite that even the maid who waited on his table, a tall, gangling girl with a vinegar face and a kind heart, worried for fear he might be sick, and added unordered delicacies to his American plan meal. He went over to Hollis Creek in the swiftest conveyance he could obtain, which was naturally an auto, but he did not have 'Ennery for his chauffeur, of which he was heartily glad, for 'Ennery might have wanted to talk.

On the porch of Hollis Creek Inn he found Princeman and Mr. Stevens in earnest conversation. He knew what that meant. Princeman was already discussing with Mr. Stevens the matter of control of the Marsh Pulp Company. Princeman rose when Sam stepped up on the porch, and strolled away from Mr. Stevens. He nodded pleasantly to Turner, and the latter, returning the nod fully as pleasantly, was about to hurry on in search of Miss Josephine, when Mr. Stevens checked him.

"Hello, Sam," he called. "I've just been waiting to see you."

"All right," said Sam. "I'll be around presently."

"No, but come here," insisted Mr. Stevens.

Sam cast a nervous glance about the grounds and along the side porch; Miss Josephine most certainly was not among those present. He still hesitated, impatient to get away.

"Just a minute, Sam," insisted Stevens. "I want to talk to you right now."

With unwilling feet Sam went over.

"Sit down," directed Stevens, pushing forward a chair.

"What is it?" asked Sam, still standing.

"I have been talking with Princeman and Westlake about your Marsh Pulp Company."

"Yes," inquired Sam nervously.

"And everybody seems to be most enthusiastic about it. Fact of the matter is, my boy, I consider it a tremendous investment opportunity. The only drawback there seems to be is in the matter of stock distribution and voting power. I want you to explain this very fully to me."

"I thought you were quite satisfied with our talk last night," returned Sam, glancing hastily over his shoulder.

"I am, in so far as the investment goes, Sam. I've promised you that I'd take a good block of stock, and you've promised to make room for me in the company. I expect to go through with that, but I want to know about this other phase of the matter before I get into any entanglements with opposing factions. Now you sit right down there and tell me about it."

Despairingly Sam sat down and proceeded briefly and concisely to explain to him the various plans of incorporation which had been proposed. Ten minutes later he almost groaned, as a trap, drawn by a pair of handsome buckskin horses, driven by Princeman and containing Miss Josephine, crunched upon the gravel driveway in front of the porch. Miss Stevens greeted Mr. Turner very heartily indeed, Princeman stopping for that purpose. Sam ran down and shook hands with her. Oh, she was most cordial; just as cordial and polite as anybody he knew!

"I did not expect you at all," she said, "but I knew you were here, for I saw you from the window as you came up the drive. Pleasant weather, isn't it? Oh, papa!"

"Yes," answered Mr. Stevens ponderously from his place on the porch.

"Up on my dresser you will find a box of candy which Mr. Turner was kind enough to have sent me, and he confesses that he has never tasted maraschino chocolates. Won't you please run up and get them and let Mr. Turner sample them?"

"Huh!" grunted Mr. Stevens. "If Sam Turner insists upon running me up two flights of stairs on an errand of that sort, I suppose I'll have to go. But he won't."

"You're lazy," she said to her father in affectionate banter, then, with a wave of her hand and a bright nod to Mr. Turner, she was gone!

Sam trudged slowly up on the porch with the heart gone entirely out of him for business; and yet, as he approached Mr. Stevens he pulled himself together with a jerk. After all, she was gone, and he could not bring her back, and in his talk with Stevens he had just approached a grave and serious situation.

"The fact of the matter is, Mr. Stevens," said he as he sat down again, "these people are the very people I want to get into my concern, but they are old hands at the stock incorporation game, and even before I've organized the company they are planning to get it out of my hands. Now it is my scheme, mine and the kid brother's, and I don't propose to allow that."

"Well, Sam," said Mr. Stevens slowly, "you know capital of late has had a lot of experience with corporate business, and it isn't the fashionable thing this year for the control and the capital to be in separate hands—right at the very beginning."

This was the signal for the struggle, and Sam plunged earnestly into the conflict. At three-fifteen he suddenly rose and made his adieus. He would have liked to stay until Miss Josephine came back, so that he could make one more desperate attempt to set himself right with her, but there was that deferred engagement with Blackrock, and reluctantly he whirled back to Meadow Brook.

CHAPTER IX.
WHEREIN SAM TURNER PROVES HIMSELF
TO BE A VIOLENT FLIRT

The rest of that week was a worried and an anxious one for Sam. He sent daily advices to his brother, and he received daily advices in return. The people upon whom he had originally counted to form the Marsh Pulp Company had set themselves coldly against the matter of control, and on comparing the apparent situation in New York with the situation at Meadow Brook, he made sure that he could secure more advantageous terms with the Princeman crowd. He spent his time in wrestling with his prospective investors both singly and in groups, but they were obdurate. They liked his company, they saw in it tremendous possibilities, but they did not intend to invest their money where they could not vote it. That was flat!

This was on the business side. About the really important matter of Miss Stevens, since his most recent bad performance, the time when he had made the special trip to see her and had spent his time in talking business with her father, he had not been able to come near her. She was always engaged. He saw her riding with Hollis; he saw her driving with Princeman; he saw her playing tennis with Billy Westlake, but the greatest boon he ever received was a nod and a pleasant word. He industriously sent her flowers. She as industriously sent him nice, polite little notes of thanks.

In the meantime, alternating with his marsh pulp wrangles, he worked like a Trojan at the athletic graces he should have cultivated in his younger days. He rode every morning; he practised every day at tennis and croquet; every evening he bowled; and every time some one sat at the piano and played dance music and the young people fell into impromptu waltzes and two-steps on the porch, he joined them and danced religiously with whomsoever he found to hand; usually Miss Hastings or Miss Westlake.

The latter ingenious young lady, during this while, continued to adore business, and with increasing fervor every day, and regretted, quite aloud, that she had never paid sufficient attention to this absorbing amusement, out of which all the men, that is, those who were really strong and purposeful, seem to derive so much satisfaction! On the following Monday at Bald Hill, when Hollis Creek and Meadow Brook fraternized together, in the annual union picnic, she found occasion for the most direct tête-à-tête of all anent commercial matters.

Under Bald Hill were any number of charming natural retreats, jumbles of Titanically toy-strewn, clean, bare rocks, screened here and there by tangles of young scrub oak and pine which grew apparently on bare stone surfaces and out of infinitesimal chinks and crannies, in utter defiance of all natural law. Go where you would on that day, there were couples in each of the rock shelters; young couples, engaged in that fascinating pastime of finding out all they could about each other, and wondering about each other, and revealing themselves to each other as much as they cared to do, and flirting; oh, in a perfectly respectable sort of a way, you know; legitimate and commendable flirting; the sort of flirting which is only experimental and necessary, and which may cease at any moment to become mere airy trifling, and turn into something intensely and desperately serious, having a vital bearing upon the entire future lives of people; and there were deeply solemn moments, in spite of all the surface hilarity and gaiety, in many of these little out of way nooks kindly provided by beneficent nature for this identical purpose.

In one of these nooks, a curious sort of doll's amphitheatre, partly screened by dwarf cedars, were Miss Westlake and Mr. Turner, and Sam could not tell you to this day how she had roped him out of the herd, and isolated him, and brought him there.

"Business is just perfectly fascinating," she was saying. "I've been talking a lot to papa about it here lately. He thinks a great deal of you, by the way."

"He does," Sam grunted in non-committal acknowledgment, with the sharp reflection that he had better look out for himself if that were the case, since the most of Westlake's old friends were bankrupt, he being the best business man of them all.

"Yes; he says you have an excellent business proposition, too, in your new Marsh Pulp Company." She said marsh pulp without an instant's hesitation.

"I think it's good myself," agreed Sam; "that is, if I can keep hold of it." Inwardly he added, "And if I can keep old Westlake's clutches off."

She laughed lightly.

"Papa mentioned that very thing," she informed him. "I don't think I quite understand what control of stock means, although I've had papa explain it to me. I gather this much, however, that it is something you want very much, but can scarcely get without some large stockholder voting his stock with you."

Sam inspected her narrowly.

"You seem to have a pretty good idea of the thing after all," he admitted, wondering how much she really knew and understood. "But maybe your father wouldn't like your repeating to me what you accidentally learned from him in conversation. Business men are usually pretty particular about that."

"Oh, he wouldn't mind at all," she said airily. "I'm having him explain a lot of things to me, because he's making separate investments for Billy and me. All his new enterprises are for us, and in the last two or three years he's turned over lots of stock to us in our own names. But I've never done any actual voting on it. I've only given proxies. I sign a little blank, you know, that papa fills out for me and shows me where to put my name and mails to somebody or other, or else takes it and votes it himself; but I'd rather vote it my own self. I should think it would be ever so much fun. I'm trying to find out about how they do such things, and I'd be very glad to have you tell me all you can about it. It's just perfectly fascinating."

"Yes, it is," Sam admitted. "So you think you may eventually own some stock in the Marsh Pulp Company?" and he became quite interested.

"If papa takes any I'm quite sure I shall," she returned; "and I think he will, from what he said. He seems to be so enthusiastic about it that I'm going to ask him for this stock, and let Billy have the next that he buys. I hope he does take a good lot of it. Isn't this the dearest place imaginable?" and with charming naïveté she looked about the tiny amphitheatre-like circle, admiring the projecting stones which formed natural seats, and the broad shelving of slippery rock which led up to it.

"Yes, it is," said Sam with considerable thoughtfulness, and once more inspected Miss Westlake critically.

There was no question that she would be as stout as her mother and her father when she reached their age. However, personal attractiveness is an essence and can not be weighed by the pound. Sam was bound to admit, after thoughtful judgment, that Miss Westlake might be personally attractive to a great many people, but really there hadn't seemed to be anything flowing from him to her or from her to him, even when he had held tightly to her hand to help her up the steep slope of the rock floor.

"Yes, it is a charming place," he once more admitted. "Looks almost as if this little semi-circle had been built out of these loose rocks by design. Of course, your father wouldn't take the original stock in your name."

"Oh, no, I don't suppose so," she said. "He never does. He takes out the stock himself, and then transfers it to us."

"Of course," Sam agreed; "and naturally he'd hold it long enough to vote at the original stock-holders' meeting."

"I couldn't say about that," she laughed. "That's going beyond my business depth just yet, but I'm going to learn all about such things," and she looked across at him with apparent shy confidence that he would take pleasure in teaching her.

"Hoo-hoo-oo-oo-oo-oo!" came a sudden call from down in the road, and, turning, they saw Miss Hastings and Billy Westlake, who both waved their hands at the amphitheatre couple and came scrambling up the rocks.

"Mr. Princeman and Mr. Tilloughby are looking for you everywhere, Hallie," said Miss Hastings to Miss Westlake. "You know you promised to make that famous salad dressing of yours. Luncheon is nearly ready, all but that, and they're waiting for you over at the glade. My, what a dear little place this is! How did you ever find it?" Miss Hastings was now quite conspicuously panting and fanning herself. "I'm so tired climbing those rocks," she went on. "I shall simply have to sit down and rest a bit. Billy will take you over, Hallie, and Mr. Turner will bring me by and by, I am sure."

Mr. Turner stated that he would do so with pleasure. Miss Westlake surveyed her dearest friend more in anger than in sorrow. It was such a brazen trick, and she gazed from her brother to Mr. Turner in sheer wonder that they were not startled into betrayal of how shocked they were. Whatever strong emotions they might have had upon that subject were utterly without reflection upon the outside, however, for Billy Westlake and Sam Turner were eying each other solely with a vacuous mutual wish of saying something decently polite and human. Mr. Turner made a desperate stab.

"I hope you're in good form for the bowling tournament to-night," he observed with self-urged anxiety. "Hollis Creek mustn't win, you know."

"I'm as near fit as usual," said Billy; "but Princeman is the chap who's going to carry off the honors for Meadow Brook. Bowled an average last night of two forty-five. I'm sorry you couldn't make the team."

"I should have started fifteen years ago to do that," said Sam with a wry smile. "I think I would get along all right, though, if they didn't have those grooves at the side of the alleys."

Billy Westlake looked at him gravely. Since Sam did not smile, this could not be a joke.

"But they are absolutely necessary, you know," he protested, as he took his sister's arm and helped her down the slope.

Miss Westlake went away entirely out of patience with the two men, and very much to Billy's surprise gave him her revised estimate of that Hastings girl. Miss Hastings, however, was in a far different frame of mind. She was an exclamation point of admiration about an endless variety of things; about the dear little amphitheatre, about how well her friend Miss Westlake was looking and how successful Hallie had been this summer in reducing, and how much Mr. Turner was improving in his tennis and croquet and riding and bowling and everything. "And, Mr. Turner, what is pulp? And do they actually make paper out of it?" she wound up.

Very gravely Mr. Turner informed her on the process of paper making, and she was a chorus of little vivacious ohs and ahs all the way through. She sat on the side of the stone circle from which she could look down the road, and she chattered on and on and on, and still on, until something she saw below warned her that she was staying an unconscionable length of time, so she rose and told Mr. Turner they must really go, and held out her hand to be helped down the slope. That was really a very slippery rock, and it was probably no fault of Miss Hastings that her feet slipped and that she had to throw herself squarely into Mr. Turner's embrace, and even throw her arm up over his shoulder to save herself. It was a staggery place, even for a sturdily muscled young man like Mr. Turner to keep his footing, and with that fair burden upon him he had to stand some little time poised there to retain his balance. Then, very gently and carefully, he turned straight about, lifting Miss Hastings entirely from her feet and setting her gravely down on the safe ledge below the sloping rock; but before he had even had time to let go of her he glanced down into the road, toward which the turn had faced him, and saw there, looking up aghast at the tableau, Mr. Princeman and Miss Stevens!

The sharp and instantly suppressed laugh of Princeman came floating up to them, but Miss Stevens turned squarely about in the direction of the glade, and being instantly joined by Princeman, they walked quietly away.

Mr. Turner suddenly found himself perspiring profusely, and was compelled to mop his brow, but Miss Hastings disdained to give any sign that anything unusual whatsoever had happened, except by walking with a limp, albeit a very slight one, as she returned to the glade. That limp comforted Mr. Turner somewhat, and, spying Miss Stevens in a little group near the tables, he was very careful to parade Miss Hastings straight over there and place her limp on display. Miss Stevens, however, walked away; no mere limp could deceive her!

Well, if she wanted to be miffed at a little accident like that, and read things falsely, and think the worst of people, she might; that was all Sam had to say about it! but what he had to say about it did not comfort him. He rather savagely "shook" Miss Hastings at his first opportunity, and Vivian's dearest friend, who had been hovering in the offing, saw him do it, which was a great satisfaction to her. Later she seized upon him, although he had savagely sworn to stick to the men, and by some incomprehensible process Sam found himself once more tête-à-tête with Miss Westlake, just over at the edge of the glade where the sumac grew. She made him gather a lot of the leaves for her, and showed him how they used to weave clover wreaths when she was a little girl, and wove one for him of sumac, and gaily crowned him with it; and just as she was putting the fool thing on his head he glanced up, and there Princeman, laughing, was just passing them a little ways off, in company with Miss Josephine Stevens!

CHAPTER X.
THE VALUE OF A PIANOLA TRAINING

On that very same evening Hollis Creek came over to the bowling tournament, and Miss Stevens, arriving with young Hollis, promptly lost that perfervid young man, who had become somewhat of a nuisance in his sentimental insistence. Mr. Turner, watching her from afar, saw her desert the calfly smitten one, and immediately dashed for the breach. He had watched from too great a distance, however, for Billy Westlake gobbled up Miss Josephine before Sam could get there, and started with her for that inevitable stroll among the brookside paths which always preceded a bowling tournament. While he stood nonplussed, looking after them, Miss Hastings glided to his side in a matter of course way.

"Isn't it a perfectly charming evening?" she wanted to know.

"It is a regular dear of an evening," admitted Sam savagely.

In his single thoughtedness he was scrambling wildly about within the interior of his skull for a pretext to get rid of Miss Hastings, but it suddenly occurred to him that now he had a legitimate excuse for following the receding couple, and promptly upon the birth of this idea, he pulled in that direction and Miss Hastings came right along, though a trifle silently. With all her vivacious chattering, she was not without shrewdness, and with no trouble whatever she divined precisely why Sam chose the path he did, and why he seemed in such almost blundering haste. They *were* a little late, it was true, for just as they started, Billy and Miss Stevens turned aside and out of sight into the shadiest and narrowest and most involved of the shrubbery-lined paths, the one which circled about the little concealed summer-house with a dovecote on top, which was commonly dubbed "the cooing place." Following down this path the rear couple suddenly came upon a tableau which made them pause abruptly. Billy Westlake, upon the steps of the summer-house, was upon his knees, there in the swiftly blackening dusk, before the appalled Miss Stevens; actually upon his knees! Silently the two watchers stole away, but when they were out of earshot Miss Hastings tittered. Sam, though the moment was a serious one for him, was also compelled to grin.

"I didn't know they did it that way any more," he confessed.

"They don't," Miss Hastings informed him; "that is, unless they are very, very young, or very, very old."

"Apparently you've had experience," observed Sam.

"Yes," she admitted a little bitterly. "I think I've had rather more than my share; but all with ineligibles."

Sam felt a trace of pity for Miss Hastings, who was of polite family, but poor, and a guest of the Westlakes, but he scarcely knew how to express it, and felt that it was not quite safe anyhow, so he remained discreetly silent.

By mutual, though unspoken impulse, they stopped under the shade of a big tree up on the lawn, and waited for the couple who had been found in the delicate situation either to reappear on the way back to the house, or to emerge at the other end of the path on the way to the bowling shed. It was scarcely three minutes when they reappeared on the way back to the house, and both watchers felt an instant thrill of relief, for the two were by no means lover-like in their attitudes. Billy had hold of Miss Josephine's arm and was helping her up the slope, but their shoulders were not touching in the process, nor were arms clasped closely against sides. They passed by the big tree unseeing, then, as they neared the house, without a word, they parted. Miss Stevens proceeded toward the porch, and stopped to take a handkerchief from her sleeve and pass it carefully and lightly over her face. Billy Westlake strode off a little way toward the bowling shed, stopped and lit a cigarette, took two or three puffs, started on, stopped again, then threw the cigarette to the ground with quite unnecessary vigor, and stamped on it. Miss Hastings, without adieus of any sort, glided swiftly away in the direction of Billy, and then a dim glimmer of understanding came to Sam Turner that only Miss Stevens had stood in the way of Miss Hastings' capture of Billy Westlake. He wasted no time over this thought, however, but strode very swiftly and determinedly up to Miss Josephine.

"I'm glad to find you alone," he said; "I want to make an explanation."

"Don't bother about it," she told him frigidly. "You owe me no explanations whatsoever, Mr. Turner."

"I'm going to make them anyhow," he declared. "You saw me twice this afternoon in utterly asinine situations."

"I remember of no such situations," she stated still frigidly, and started to move on toward the house.

"But wait a minute," said Sam, catching her by the arm and detaining her. "You did see me in silly situations, and I want you to know the facts about them."

"I'm not at all interested," she informed him, now with absolute north pole iciness, and started to move away again.

He held her more tightly.

"The first time," he went on, "was when Miss Hastings slipped on the rocks and I had to catch her to keep her from falling."

"Will you kindly let me go, Mr. Turner?" demanded Miss Josephine.

"No, I will not!" he replied, and pulled her about a trifle so that she was compelled to face him. "I don't choose to have anybody, least of all you, think wrongly of me."

"Mr. Turner, I do not choose to be detained against my will," declared Miss Josephine.

"Mr. Turner," boomed a deep-timbered voice right behind them, "the lady has requested you to let her go. I should advise you to do so."

Mr. Turner was attempting to frame up a reasonable answer to this demand when Miss Josephine prevented him from doing so.

"Mr. Princeman," said she to the interrupting gallant, "I thank you for your interference on my behalf, but I am quite capable of protecting myself," and leaving the two stunned gentlemen together, she once more took her handkerchief from her sleeve and walked swiftly up to the porch, brushing the handkerchief lightly over her face again.

"Well, I'll be damned!" said Princeman, looking after her in more or less bewilderment.

"So will I," said Sam. "Have you a cigarette about you?"

Princeman gave him one and they took a light from the same match, then, neither one of them caring to discuss any subject whatever at that particular moment, they separated, and Sam hunted a lonely corner. He wanted to be alone and gloom. Confound bowling, anyhow! It was a dull and uninteresting game. He cared less for it as time went on, he found; less to-night than ever. He crept away into the dim and deserted parlor and sat down at the piano, the only friend in which he cared to confide just then. He played, with a queer lingering touch which had something of hesitation in it, and which reduced all music to a succession of soft chords, *The Maid of Dundee* and *Annie Laurie*, *The Banks of Banna* and *The Last Rose of Summer*, then one of the simpler nocturnes of Chopin, and, following these, a quaint, slow melody which was like all of the others and yet like none.

"Bravo!" exclaimed a gentle voice in the doorway, and he turned, startled, to see Miss Stevens standing there. She did not explain why she had relented, but came directly into the room and stood at the end of the piano. He reached up and shook hands with her quite naturally, and just as naturally and simply she let her hand lie in his for an instant. How soft and warm her palm was, and how grateful the touch of it!

"What a pleasant surprise!" she said. "I didn't know you played."

"I don't," he confessed, smiling. "If you had stopped to listen you would have known. You ought to hear my kid brother play though. He's a corker."

"But I did listen," she insisted, ignoring the reference to his "kid brother." "I stood there a long time and I thought it beautiful. What was that last selection?"

He flushed guiltily.

"It was—oh, just a little thing I sort of put together myself," he told her.

"How delightful! And so you compose, too?"

"Not at all," he hastily assured her. "This is the only thing, and it seemed to come just sort of naturally to me from time to time. I don't suppose it's finished yet, because I never play it exactly as I did before. I always seem to add a little bit to it. I do wish that I had had time to know more of music. What little I play I learned from a pianola."

"A what?" she gasped.

He laughed in a half-embarrassed way.

"A pianola," he repeated. "You see I've always been hungry for music, and while my kid brother was still in college I began to be able to afford things, and one of the first luxuries was a pianola. You know the machine has a little lever which throws the keys in or out of engagement, so that you can play it as a regular piano if you wish, and if you leave the keys engaged while you are playing the rolls, they work up and down; so by watching these I gradually learned to pick out my favorite tunes by hand. I couldn't play them so well by myself as the rolls played them, but somehow or other they gave me more satisfaction."

Miss Stevens did not laugh. In some indefinable way all this made a difference in Sam Turner—a considerable difference—and she felt quite justified in having deliberately come to the conclusion that she had been "mean" to him; in having deliberately slipped away from the others as they were all going over to the bowling alleys; in having come back deliberately to find him.

"Your favorite tunes," she repeated musingly. "What was the first one, I wonder? One of those that you have just been playing?"

"The first one?" he returned with a smile. "No, it was a sort of rag-time jingle. I thought it very pretty then, but I played it over the other day, the first time in years, and I didn't seem to like it at all. In fact, I wonder how I ever did like it."

Rag-time! And now, left entirely to his own devices and for his own pleasure, he was playing Chopin! Yes, it made quite a difference in Sam Turner. She was glad that she had decided to wear his roses, glad even that he recognized them. At her solicitation Sam played again the plaintive little air of his own composition—and played it much better than ever he had played it before. Then they walked out on the porch and strolled down toward the bowling shed. Half way there was a little side path, leading off through an arbor into a shady way which crossed the brook on a little rustic bridge, which wound about between flowerbeds and shrubbery and back by another little bridge, and which lengthened the way to the bowling shed by about four times the normal distance—and they took that path; and when they reached the bowling alley they were not quite ready to go in.

There seemed no reasonable excuse for staying out longer, however, for the bowling had already started, and, moreover, young Tilloughby happened to come to the door and spied them. Princeman was just getting up to bowl for the honor and glory of Meadow Brook, and within one minute later Miss Stevens was watching the handsome young paper manufacturer with absorbed interest. He was a fine picture of athletic manhood as he stood up, weighing the ball, and a splendid picture of masculine action as he rushed forward to deliver it. Sam had to acknowledge that himself, and out of fairness he even had to join in the mad applause when Princeman made strike after strike. They had Princeman up again in the last frame, and it was a ticklish moment. The Hollis Creek team was fifty points ahead. Dramatic unities, under the circumstances, demanded that Princeman, by a tremendous exercise of coolness and skill, overcome that lead by his own personal efforts, and he did, winning the tournament for Meadow Brook with a breathless few points to spare.

But did Sam Turner care that Princeman was the hero of the hour? More power to Princeman, for from the bevy of flushed and eager girls who flocked about the Adonis-like victor, Miss Josephine Stevens was absent. She was there, with him, in Paradise! Incidentally Sam made an engagement to drive with her in the morning, and when, at the close of that delightful evening, the carryall carried her away, she beamed upon him; gave him two or three beams in fact, and said good-by personally and waved her hand to him personally; nobody else was there in all that crowd but just they two!

CHAPTER XI.
THE WESTLAKES DECIDE TO INVEST

Miss Hastings did not exactly snub Sam in the morning, but she was surprisingly indifferent to him after all her previous cordiality, and even went so far as to forget the early morning constitutional she was to have taken with him; instead she passed him coolly by on the porch right after an extremely early breakfast, and sauntered away down lovers' lane, arm in arm with Billy Westlake, who was already looking very much comforted. Sam, who had been dreading that walk, released it with a sigh of intense satisfaction, planning that in the interim until time for his drive, he would improve his tennis a bit with Miss Westlake. He was just hunting her up when he met Bob Tilloughby, who invited him to join a riding party from both houses for a trip over to Sunset Rock.

"Sorry," said Sam with secret satisfaction, "but I've an engagement over at Hollis Creek at ten o'clock," and Tilloughby carried that information back to Miss Westlake, who had sent him.

An engagement at Hollis Creek at ten o'clock, eh? Well, Miss Westlake knew who that meant; none other than her dear friend, Josephine Stevens! Being a young lady of considerable directness, she went immediately to her father.

"Have you definitely made up your mind, pop, to take stock in Mr. Turner's company?" she asked, sitting down by that placid gentleman.

Without removing his interlocked hands from their comfortable resting-place in plain sight, he slowly twirled his thumbs some three times, and then stopped.

"Yes, I think I shall," he said.

"About how much?" Miss Westlake wanted to know.

"Oh, about twenty-five thousand."

"Who's to get it?"

"Why, I thought I'd divide it between Billy and you."

Miss Westlake put her hand on her father's arm.

"Say, pop, give it to me, please," she pleaded. "Billy can take the next stock you buy, or I'll let him have some of my other in exchange."

Mr. Westlake surveyed his daughter out of a pair of fish-gray eyes without turning his head.

"You seem to be especially interested in this stock. You asked about it yesterday and Sunday and one day last week."

"Yes, I am," she admitted. "It's a really first-class business investment, isn't it?"

"Yes, I think it is," replied Westlake; "as good as any stock in an untried company can be, anyhow. At least it's an excellent investment chance."

"That's what I thought," she said. "I'm judging, of course, only by what you say, and by my impression of Mr. Turner. It seems to me that almost anything he goes into should be highly successful."

Mr. Westlake slowly whirled his thumbs in the other direction, three separate twirls, and stopped them.

"Yes," he agreed. "I'm investing the money in just Sam myself, although the scheme itself looks like a splendid one."

Miss Westlake was silent a moment while she twisted at the button on her father's coat sleeve.

"I don't quite understand this matter of stock control," she went on presently. "You've explained it to me, but I don't seem quite to get the meaning of it."

"Well, it's like this," explained Mr. Westlake. "Sam Turner, with only a paltry investment, say about five thousand dollars, wants to be able to dictate the entire policy of a million-dollar concern. In other words, he wants a majority of stock, which will let him come into the stock-holders' meetings, and vote into office his own board of directors, who will do just what he says; and if he wanted to he might have them vote the entire profits of the concern for his salary."

"But, father, he wouldn't do anything like that," she protested, shocked.

"No, he probably wouldn't," admitted Mr. Westlake, "but I wouldn't be wise to let him have the chance, just the same."

"But, father," objected Miss Hallie, after further thought, "it's his invention, you know, and his process, and if he doesn't have control couldn't all you other stock-holders get together and appropriate the profits yourselves?"

Mr. Westlake gave his thumbs one quick turn.

"Yes," he grudgingly confessed. "In fact, it's been done," and there was a certain grim satisfaction at the corners of his mouth which his daughter could not interpret, as he thought back over the long list of absorptions which had made old Bill Westlake the power that he was.

"But—but, father," and she hesitated a long time.

"Yes," he encouraged her.

"Even if you won't let him have enough stock to obtain control, if some one other person should own enough of the stock, couldn't they put their stock with his and let him do just about as he liked?"

"Oh, yes," agreed Mr. Westlake without any twirling of his thumbs at all; "that's been done, too."

"Would this twenty-five thousand dollars' worth of stock that you're buying, pop, if it were added to what you men are willing to let Mr. Turner have, give him control?"

Again Mr. Westlake turned his speculative gray eyes upon his daughter and gave her a long, careful scrutiny, which she received with downcast lashes.

"No," he replied.

"How much would?"

"Well, fifty thousand would do it."

"Say, pop—"

"Yes."

Another long interval.

"I wish you'd buy fifty thousand for me in place of twenty-five."

"Humph," grunted Mr. Westlake, and after one sharp glance at her he looked down at his big fat thumbs and twirled them for a long, long time. "Well," said he, "Sam Turner is a fine young man. I've known him in a business way for five or six years, and I never saw a flaw in him of any sort. All right. You give Billy your sugar stock and I'll buy you this fifty thousand."

Miss Westlake reached over and kissed her father impulsively.

"Thanks, pop," she said. "Now there's another thing I want you to do."

"What, more?" he demanded.

"Yes, more," and this time the color deepened in her cheeks. "I want you to hunt up Mr. Turner and tell him that you're going to take that much."

Mr. Westlake with a smile reached up and pinched his daughter's cheek.

"Very well, Hallie, I'll do it," said he.

She patted him affectionately on the bald spot.

"Good for you," she said. "Be sure you see him this morning, though, and before half-past nine."

"You're particular about that, eh?"

"Yes, it's rather important," she admitted, and blushed furiously.

Westlake patted his daughter on the shoulder.

"Hallie," said He, "if Billy only had your common-sense business instinct, I wouldn't ask for anything else in this world; but Billy is a saphead."

Mr. Westlake, thinking that he understood the matter very thoroughly, though in reality overunderstanding it—nice word, that—took it upon himself with considerable seriousness to hunt up Sam Turner; but it was fully nine-thirty before he found that energetic young man. Sam was just going down the driveway in a neat little trap behind a team of spirited grays.

"Wait a minute, Sam, wait a minute," hailed Westlake, puffing laboriously across the closely cropped lawn.

Sam held up his horses abruptly, and they stood swinging their heads and champing at their bits, while Sam, with a trace of a frown, looked at his watch.

"What's your rush?" asked Westlake. "I've been hunting for you everywhere. I want to talk about some important features of that Marsh Pulp Company of yours."

"All right," said Sam. "I'm open for conversation. I'll see you right after lunch."

"No. I must see you now," insisted Westlake. "I've—I've got to decide on some things right this morning. I—I've got to know how to portion out my investments."

Sam looked at his watch and was genuinely distressed.

"I'm sorry," said he, "but I have an engagement over at Hollis Creek at exactly ten o'clock, and I've scant time to make it."

"Business?" demanded Westlake.

"No," confessed Sam slowly.

"Oh, social then. Well, social engagements in America always play second fiddle to business ones, and don't you forget it. I'll talk about this matter this morning or I won't talk about it at all."

Sam stopped nonplussed. Westlake was an important factor in the prospective Marsh Pulp Company.

"Tell you what you do," said he, after some quick thought. "Why can't you get in the trap and drive over to Hollis Creek with me? We can talk on the way and you can visit with your friends over there until time for luncheon; then I'll bring you back and we can talk on the way home, too."

Miss Hallie and Princeman and young Tilloughby came cantering down the drive and waved hands at the two men.

"All right," said Westlake decisively, looking after his daughter and answering her glance with a nod. "Wait until I get my hat," and he wheeled abruptly away.

Sam fumed and fretted and jerked his watch back and forth from his pocket, while Westlake wasted fifteen precious minutes in waddling up to the house and hunting for his hat and returning with it, and two minutes more in bungling his awkward way into the buggy; then Sam started the grays at such a terrific pace that, until they came to the steep hill midway of the course, there was no chance for conversation. While the horses pulled up this steep hill, however, Westlake had his opportunity.

"I suppose you know," he said, "that you're not going to be allowed over two thousand shares of common stock for your patents."

"I'm beginning to give up the hope of having more," admitted Sam. "However, I'm going to stick it out to the last ditch."

"It won't be permitted, so you might as well give up that idea. How much stock do you think of buying?"

"About five thousand dollars' worth of the preferred," said Sam.

"Which will give you fifty bonus shares of the common. I suppose of course you figure on eventually securing control in some way or other."

"Not being an infant, I do," returned Sam, flicking his whip at a weed and gathering his lines up quickly as the mettled horses jumped.

"I don't know of any one person who's going to buy enough stock to help you out in that plan; unless I should do it myself," suggested Westlake, and waited.

Sam surveyed the other man long and silently. Westlake, as the largest minority shareholder, had done some very strange things to corporations in his time.

"Neither do I," said Sam non-committally.

There was another long silence.

"If you carry through this Marsh Pulp Company to a successful termination, you will be fairly well fixed for a young man, won't you?" the older man ventured by and by.

"Well," hesitated Sam, "I'll have a start anyhow."

"I should say you would," Westlake assured him, placing his hands in his favorite position for contemplative discussion. "You'll have a good enough start to enable you to settle down."

"Yes," admitted Sam.

"What you need, my boy, is a wife," went on Mr. Westlake. "No man's business career is properly assured until he has a wife to steady him down."

"I believe that," agreed Sam. "I've come to the same conclusion myself, and to tell you the truth of the matter I've been contemplating marriage very seriously since I've been down here."

"Good!" approved Westlake. "You're a fine boy, Sam. I may tell you right now that I approve of both you and your decision very heartily. I rather thought there was something in the wind that way."

"Yes," confessed Sam hesitantly. "I don't mind admitting that I have even gone so far as to pick out the girl, if she'll have me."

Mr. Westlake smiled.

"I don't think there will be any trouble on that score," said he. "Of course, Sam, I'm not going to force your confidence, or anything of that sort, but—but I want to tell you that I think you're all right," and he very solemnly shook hands with Mr. Turner.

They had just reached the top of the hill when Westlake again returned to business.

"I'm glad to know you're going to settle down, Sam," he said. "It inspires me with more confidence in your affairs, and I may say that I stand ready to subscribe, in my daughter's name, for fifty thousand dollars' worth of the stock of your company."

"Well," said Sam, giving the matter careful weight. "It will be a good investment for her."

Before Mr. Westlake had any time to reply to this, the grays, having just passed the summit of the hill, leaped forward in obedience to another swish of Sam's whip.

CHAPTER XII.
ANOTHER MISSED APPOINTMENT

The trio from Meadow Brook, on their way to Sunset Rock galloped up to the Hollis Creek porch, and, finding Miss Stevens there, gaily demanded that she accompany them.

"I'm sorry," said Miss Stevens, who was already in driving costume, "but I have an engagement at ten o'clock," and she looked back through the window into the office, where the clock then stood at two minutes of the appointed time; then she looked rather impatiently down the driveway, as she had been doing for the past five minutes.

"Well, at least you'll come back to the bar with us and have an ice-cream cocktail," insisted Princeman, reining up close to the porch and putting his hand upon the rail in front of her.

"I don't see how I can refuse that," said Miss Stevens with a smile and another glance down at the driveway, "although it's really a little early in the day to begin drinking," and she waited for them to dismount, going back with them into the little ice-cream parlor and "soft drink" and confectionery dispensary which had been facetiously dubbed "the bar." Here she was careful to secure a seat where she could look out of the window down toward the road, and also see the clock.

After a weary while, during which Miss Josephine had undergone a variety of emotions which she was very careful not to mention, the party rose from the discussion of their ice-cream soda and the bowling tournament and all the various other social interests of the two resorts, and made ready to depart, Miss Westlake twining her arm about the waist of her friend Miss Stevens as they emerged on the porch.

"Well, anyway, we've made you forget your engagement," Miss Westlake gaily boasted, "for you said it was to be at ten, and now it's ten-thirty."

"Yes, I noticed the time," admitted Miss Stevens, rather grudgingly.

"I'm sorry we dragged you away," commiserated Miss Westlake with a swift change of tone. "Probably the party of the second part didn't know where to find you."

"No, it couldn't be anything like that," decided Miss Josephine after a thoughtful pause. "Did you see anything of Mr. Turner this morning?" she asked with sudden resolve.

"Mr. Turner," repeated Miss Westlake in well-feigned surprise. "Why, yes, I know papa said early this morning that he was going to have a business talk with Mr. Turner, and as we left Meadow Brook papa was just going after his hat to take a drive with him."

"I wonder if it would be an imposition to ask you to wait about five minutes longer," inquired Miss Stevens with a languidness which did *not* deceive. "I think I can change to my riding-habit almost within that time."

"We'll be delighted to wait," asserted Miss Westlake eagerly, herself looking apprehensively down the driveway; "won't we, boys?"

"Sure; what is it?" returned Princeman.

"Josephine says that if we'll wait five minutes longer she'll go with us."

"We'll wait an hour if need be," declared Princeman gallantly.

"It won't need be," said Miss Stevens lightly, and hurrying into the office she ordered the clerk to send for her saddle-horse.

For ten interminable minutes Miss Westlake never took her eyes from the road, at the end of which time Miss Stevens returned, hatted and habited and booted and whipped.

The Hollis Creek young lady was rather grim as she rode down the graveled approach beside Miss Westlake, and both the girls cast furtive glances behind them as they turned away from the Meadow Brook road. When they were safely out of sight around the next bend, Miss Westlake laughed.

"Mr. Turner is such a funny person," said she. "He's liable at any moment to forget all about everything and everybody if somebody mentions business to him. If he ever takes time to get married he'll make it a luncheon hour appointment."

Even Miss Josephine laughed.

"And even then," she added, by way of elaboration, "the bride is likely to be left waiting at the church." There was a certain snap and crackle to whatever Miss Stevens said just now, however, which indicated a perturbed and even an angry state of mind.

Ten minutes later, Sam Turner, hatless, and carrying a buggy whip and wearing a torn coat, trudged up the Hollis Creek Inn drive, afoot, and walked rapidly into the office.

"Is Miss Stevens about?" he wanted to know.

"Not at present," the clerk informed him. "She ordered out her horse a few minutes ago, and started over to Sunset Rock with a party of young people from Meadow Brook."

"Which way is Sunset Rock?"

The clerk handed him a folder which contained a map of the roadways thereabouts, and pointed out the way.

"Could you get me a saddle-horse right away?"

The clerk pounded a bell and ordered up a saddle-horse for Mr. Turner, who immediately thereupon turned to the telephone, and, calling up Meadow Brook, instructed the clerk at that resort to send a carriage for Mr. Westlake, who was sitting in the trap, entirely unharmed but disinclined to walk, at the foot of Laurel Hill; then he explained that the grays had run away down this steep declivity, that the yoke bar had slipped, the tongue had fallen to the ground, had broken, and had run back up through the body of the carriage. The horses had jerked the doubletree loose, and the last he had seen of their marks they had turned up the Bald Hill road and were probably going yet. By the time he had repeated and amplified this explanation enough to beat it all through the head of the man at the other end of the wire, his horse was ready for him, and very much to the wonderment of the clerk he started off at a rattling gait, without taking the trouble either to have himself dusted or to pin up his badly torn pocket.

He only lost his way once among the devious turns which led to Sunset Rock, and arrived there just as the party, quite satisfied with the inspection of a view they had seen a score of times before, were ready to depart, his appearance upon the scene with the telltale pocket being greatly to the discomfiture of everybody concerned except Miss Stevens, who found herself unaccountably pleased that Sam's delay had been due to an accident, and able to believe his briefly told explanation at once. Miss Westlake was in despair. She had really hoped, and believed, that Sam had forgotten his engagement in business talk, and she had felt quite triumphant about it. Tilloughby, satisfied to be with Miss Westlake, and Princeman, more than content to ride by the side of Miss Stevens, were neither of them overjoyed at the appearance of the fifth rider, who made fully as much a crowd as any "third party" has ever done; and he disarranged matters considerably, for, though at first lagging behind alone, a narrow place in the road shifted the party so that when they emerged upon the other side of it Miss Westlake was riding by the side of Sam, and Tilloughby was left to ride alone in the center. Thereupon Miss Westlake's horse developed a sudden inclination to go very slowly.

"Papa says I'm becoming a very keen business woman," she remarked, by and by.

"Well, you've the proper blood in you for it," said Sam.

"That doesn't seem to count," she laughed; "look at Billy. But I think I did a remarkably clever stroke this morning. I induced papa to say he'd double his stock in your company and give it to me. He tells me I've enough to 'swing' control. Isn't that jolly?"

"It's hilariously jolly," admitted Sam, but with an inward wince. Control and Westlake were two words which did not make, for him, a cheerful juxtaposition.

"So now you'll have to be very nice indeed to me," went on Miss Westlake banteringly, "or I'm likely to vote with the other crowd."

"I'll be just as nice to you as I know how," offered Sam. "Just state what you want me to do and I'll do it."

Miss Westlake did not state what she wanted him to do. In place of that she whipped up her horse rather smartly, after a thoughtful silence, and joined Tilloughby, the three of them riding abreast. The next shifting, around a deep mud hole which only left room for an Indian file procession, brought Sam alongside Miss Josephine, and here he stuck for the balance of the ride, leaving Princeman to ride part of the time alone between the two couples, and part of the time to be the third rider with each couple in alternation. Miss Josephine was very much concerned about Mr. Turner's accident, very happy to know how lucky he had been to come off without a scratch, except for the tear in his coat, and very solicitous indeed about any further handling of the obstreperous gray team; and, forgiving him readily under the circumstances, she renewed her engagement to drive with him the next morning!

Sam rode on home at the side of Miss Westlake, after leaving Miss Stevens at Hollis Creek, in a strange and nebulous state of elation, which continued until bedtime. As he was about to retire he was handed a wire from his brother:

"Just received patent papers meet me at Restview morning train."

CHAPTER XIII.
A PLEASURE RIDE WITH MISS STEVENS

The morning train was due at ten o'clock. At ten o'clock also Sam was due at Hollis Creek to take his long deferred drive with Miss Stevens. It was a slight conflict, her engagement, but the solution to that was very easy. As early in the morning as he dared, Sam called up Miss Josephine.

"I've some glorious news," he said hopefully. "My kid brother will arrive at Restview on the ten o'clock train."

"You are to be congratulated," Miss Stevens told him, with an echo of his own delight.

"But you know we've an engagement to go driving at ten o'clock," he reminded her, still hopefully, but trembling in spirit.

There was an instant of hesitation, which ended in a laugh.

"Don't let that interfere," she said. "We can defer our drive until some other time, when fate is not so determined against it."

"But that doesn't suit me at all," he assured her. "Why can't you be ready at nine in place of ten, let me call for you at that time and drive over to Restview with me to meet Jack?"

"Is that his name?" she asked in blissfully reassuring tones. "You've never spoken of him as anybody but your 'kid brother.' Why of course I'll drive over to Restview with you. I shall be delighted to meet him."

Privately she had her own fears of what Jack Turner might turn out to be like. Sam was always so good in speaking of him, always held him in such tender regard, such profound admiration, that she feared he might prove to be perfect only in Sam's eyes.

"Good," said Sam. "Just for that I'm going to bring you over some choice blooms that I have been having the gardener save back for me," and he turned away from the telephone quite happy in the thought that for once he had been able to kill two birds with one stone without ruffling the feathers of either.

Armed with a huge consignment of brilliant blossoms, enough to transform her room into a fairy bower, he sped quite happily to Hollis Creek.

"Oh, gladiolas!" cried Miss Josephine, as he drove up. "How did you ever guess it! That little bird must have been busy again."

"Honestly, it was the little bird this time. I just had an intuition that you must like them because I do so well," upon which naïve statement Miss Josephine merely smiled, and calling her father with pretty peremptoriness, she loaded that heavy gentleman down with the flowers and with instructions concerning them, and then stepped brightly into the tonneau with Sam.

It was a pleasant ride they had to Restview, and it was a pleasant surprise which greeted Miss Josephine when the train arrived, for out of it stepped a youth who was unmistakably a Turner. He was as tall as Sam, but slighter, and as clean a looking boy as one would find in a day's journey. There was that, too, in the hand-clasp between the brothers which proclaimed at once their flawless relationship.

Miss Stevens was so relieved to find the younger Turner so presentable that she took him into her friendship at once. He was that kind of chap anyhow, and in the very first greeting she almost found herself calling him Jack. Just behind him, however, was a little, dried-up man with a complexion the color of old parchment, with sandy, stubby hair shot with gray, and a stubby gray beard shot with red. His lips were a wide straight line, as grim as judgment day. He walked with a slight stoop, but with a quick staccato step which betokened great nervous energy, a quality which the alert expression of his beady eyes confirmed with distinct emphasis.

"Hello, Creamer!" hailed Sam to this gentleman. "I didn't expect to see you here quite so soon."

"You had every right to expect me," snapped the little man querulously. "After all the experimenting I have done for you boys, you had every reason to keep me posted on all your movements; and yet I reckon if I hadn't been in your office yesterday evening when Jack said he was coming down here, you would not have notified me until you had your company all formed. Then I suppose you'd have written to tell me how much stock you had assigned to me. I'm going to be in on the formation of this company, and I'm going to have my say about it!"

"Will you never get over that dyspepsia?" chided Sam easily. "There was no intention of leaving you out."

"Just what I told him," declared Jack, turning from Miss Stevens to them. "I have been swearing to him that as soon as we had found out to-day what we were to do I would have wired him at once."

"You were quite right, Jack," approved Sam, opening the door of the car for them, "and as a proof of it, Creamer, when you return to your office you will find there a letter postmarked yesterday, telling you our exact progress here, and warning you to be in readiness to come on telegram."

"All right, then," said Mr. Creamer, somewhat mollified, "but since that letter's there and I'm here, you might as well tell me what you've done."

Sam stopped the proceedings long enough to introduce Creamer to Miss Stevens after he had closed the door upon them and had taken his own seat by the chauffeur.

"All right," he then said to Mr. Creamer, "I'll begin at the beginning."

He began at the beginning. He told Mr. Creamer all the steps in the development of the company. He detailed to him the names of the gentlemen concerned, and their complete commercial histories, pausing to answer many pertinent side questions and observations from his younger brother, who proved to be as keen a student of business puzzles as Sam himself.

"That's all very well," said Mr. Creamer, "and now I'm here. I want to get away to-night: Can't we form that company to-day? At what figure do you propose offering the original stock?"

"The preferred at fifty, with a par value of a hundred," returned Sam promptly.

"Common?" asked Mr. Creamer crisply.

"One share of common with each two shares of preferred."

"Eh! Well, I've twenty-five thousand dollars to put into this marsh pulp business, if I can have any figure in the management. I want on the board."

"It's quite likely you'll be on the board," returned Sam. "We shall have a very small list of subscribers, and the board will not be unwieldy if every investor is a director."

"Voting power in the common stock?"

"In the common stock," repeated Sam.

"Do you intend to buy any preferred?" asked Creamer.

"A hundred shares."

"How much common do you expect to take out for your patents?"

"Two hundred and fifty thousand," Sam answered without an instant's hesitation.

"Never!" exclaimed Mr. Creamer. "The time for that's gone by, young man, no matter how good your proposition is. It's too old a game. You won't handle my money with control in your hands. I have no objection to letting you have two hundred thousand dollars worth of common stock out of the half million, because that will give you an incentive to make the common worth par; but you shan't at any time have or be able to acquire a share over two hundred and forty-nine thousand; not if I know anything about it! Can you call a meeting as soon as we get there?"

"I think so," replied Sam, with a more or less worried air. "I'll try it. Tell you what I'll do. I'll run right on over to get Mr. Stevens, who wants to join the company, and in the meantime Mr. Westlake or Princeman can round up the others."

For the first time in that drive Miss Stevens had something to say, but she said it with a briefness that was like a dash of cold water to the preoccupied Sam.

"Father is over there now, I think," she said.

"Good," approved Mr. Creamer. "We can have a little direct business talk and wind up the whole affair before lunch. What time do we arrive at Meadow Brook?"

"Before eleven o'clock."

"That will give us two hours. Two hours is enough to form any company, when everybody knows exactly what he wants to do. Got a lawyer over there?"

"One of the best in the country."

Miss Stevens sat in the center seat of the tonneau. Sam, in addressing his remarks to the others and in listening to their replies, was compelled to sweep his glance squarely across her, and occasionally in these sweeps he paused to let his gaze rest upon her. She was a relief to his eyes, a blessing to them! Miss Stevens, however, seldom met any of these glances. Very much preoccupied she was, looking at the passing scenery and not seeing it.

There had begun boiling and seething in Miss Stevens a feeling that she was decidedly *de trop*, that these men could talk their absorbing business more freely if she were not there; not because she embarrassed them, but because she used up space! Nobody seemed to give her a thought. Nobody seemed to be aware that she was present. They were almost gaspingly engrossed in something far more important to them than she was. It was uncomplimentary, to say the least. She was not used to playing "second fiddle" in any company. She was in the habit of absorbing the most of the attention in her immediate vicinity. Mr. Princeman or Mr. Hollis would neither one ignore her in that way, to say nothing of Billy Westlake.

She was glad when they reached Meadow Brook. Their whole talk had been of marsh pulp, and company organization, and preferred and common stock, and who was to get it, and how much they were to pay for it, and how they were going to cut the throats of the wood pulp manufacturers, and how much profit they were going to make from the consumers and with all that, not a word for her. Not a single word! Not even an apology! Oh, it was atrocious! As soon as they drew up to the porch she rose, and before Sam could jump down to open the door of the tonneau she had opened it for herself and sprung out.

"I'll hunt up father right away for you," she stated courteously. "Glad to have met you, Mr. Creamer. I presume I shall meet you again, Mr. Turner," she said to Jack. "Thank you so much for the ride," she said to Sam, and then she was gone.

Sam looked after her blankly. It couldn't be possible that she was "huffy" about this business talk. Why, couldn't the girl see that this had to do with the birth of a great big company, a million dollar corporation, and that it was of vital importance to him? It meant the apex of a lifetime of endeavor. It meant the upbuilding of a fortune. Couldn't she see that he and his brother were two lone youngsters against all these shrewd business men, whose only terms of aiding them and floating this big company was to take their mastery of it away from them? Couldn't she understand what control of a million dollar organization meant? He was not angry with Miss Stevens for her apparent attitude in this matter, but he was hurt. He was not impatient with her, but he was impatient of the fact that she could not appreciate. Now the fat was in the fire again. He felt that. Under other circumstances he would have said that it was much more trouble than it was worth to keep in the good graces of a girl, but under the present circumstances—well, his heart had sunk down about a foot out of place, and he had a sort of faint feeling in the region of his stomach. He was just about sick. He followed her in, just in time to see the flutter of her skirts at the top of the stairway, but he could not call without making himself and her ridiculous. Confound things in general!

Mr. Stevens joined him while he was still looking into that blank hole in the world.

"Glad I happened to be here, Sam," said Stevens. "Jo tells me that your brother and Mr. Creamer have arrived and that you want to form that company right away."

"Yes," admitted Sam. "Was she sarcastic about it?"

Mr. Stevens closed his eyes and laughed.

"Not exactly sarcastic," he stated; "but she did allude to your proposed corporation as 'that old company!'"

"I was afraid so," said Sam ruefully.

Stevens surveyed him in amusement for a moment, and then in pity.

"Never mind, my boy," he said kindly. "You'll get used to these things by and by. It took me the first five years of my married life to convince Mrs. Stevens that business was not a rival to her affections, when, if I'd only have known the recipe, I could have convinced her at the start."

"How did you finally do it?" asked Sam, vitally interested.

"Made her my confidante and adviser," stated Stevens, smiling reminiscently.

Sam shook his head.

"Was that safe?" he asked. "Didn't she sometimes let out your secrets?"

"Bosh!" exclaimed Stevens. "I'd rather trust a woman than a man, any day, with a secret, business or personal. That goes for any woman; mother, sister, sweetheart, wife, daughter, or stenographer. Just give them a chance to get interested in your game, and they're with you against the world."

"Thanks," said Sam, putting that bit of information aside for future pondering. "By the way, Mr. Stevens, before we join the others I'd like to ask you how much stock you're going to carry in the Marsh Pulp Company."

"Well," returned Mr. Stevens slowly, "I did think that if the thing looked good on final analysis, I might invest twenty-five thousand dollars."

"Can't you stretch that to fifty?"

"Can't see it. But why? Don't you think you're going to fill your list?"

"We'll fill our list all right," returned Sam. "As a matter of fact, that's what I'm afraid of. These fellows are going to pool their stock, and hold control in their own hands. Now if I could get you to invest fifty thousand and vote with me under proper emergency, I could control the thing; and I ought to. It is my own company. Seems to me these fellows are selfish about it. You think I'm a good business man, don't you?"

"I certainly do," agreed Mr. Stevens emphatically.

"Well, it stands to reason that if I have two hundred and sixty thousand dollars of common stock that isn't worth a picayune unless I make it worth par, I'll hustle; and if I make my common stock worth par, I'm making a fine, fat profit for these other fellows, to say nothing of the raising of their preferred stock from the value of fifty to a hundred dollars a share, and their common from nothing to a hundred."

"That's all right, Sam," returned Mr. Stevens; "but you'll work just as hard to make your common worth par if you only have two hundred thousand; and there's a growing tendency on the part of capital to be able to keep a string on its own money. Strange, but true."

"All right," said Sam wearily. "We won't argue that point any more just now; but will you invest fifty thousand?"

"I can't promise," said Stevens, and he walked out on the porch. Much worried, Sam followed him, and with many misgivings he introduced Mr. Stevens to his brother Jack and to Mr. Creamer. The prospective organizers of the Marsh Pulp Company were already in solemn conclave on the porch, with the single exception of Princeman, who was on the lawn talking most perfunctorily with Miss Josephine. That young lady, with wickedness of the deepest sort in her soul, was doing her best to entice Mr. Princeman into forgetting the important meeting, but as soon as Princeman saw the gathering hosts he gently but firmly tore himself away, very much to her surprise and indignation. Why, he had been as rude to her as Sam Turner himself, in placing the charms of business above her own! Immediately afterward she snubbed Billy Westlake unmercifully. Had he the qualities which would go to make a successful man in any walk of life? No!

CHAPTER XIV.
A DUAL QUESTION OF MATRIMONIAL ELIGIBILITY AND STOCK SUBSCRIPTION

Mr. Westlake dropped back with his old friend Stevens as they trailed into the parlor which Blackstone had secured.

"Are you going to subscribe rather heavily in the company, Stevens?" inquired Westlake, with the curiosity of a man who likes to have his own opinion corroborated by another man of good judgment.

"Well," replied the father of Miss Josephine, "I think of taking a rather solid little block of stock. I believe I can spare twenty-five thousand dollars to invest in almost any company Sam Turner wants to start."

"He's a fine boy," agreed Westlake. "A square, straight young fellow, a good business man, and a hustler. I see him playing tennis with my girl every day, and she seems to think a lot of him."

"He's bound to make his mark," Mr. Stevens acquiesced, sharply suppressing a fool impulse to speak of his own daughter. "Do you fellows intend to let him secure control of this company?"

"I should say not!" replied Westlake, with such unnecessary emphasis that Stevens looked at him with sudden suspicion. He knew enough about old Westlake to "copper" his especially emphatic statements.

"Are you agreeable to Princeman's plan to pool all stock but Turner's?"

"Well—we can talk about that later."

"Huh!" grunted Mr. Stevens, and together the two heavy-weights, Stevens with his aggressive beard suddenly pointed a trifle more straight out, and Mr. Westlake with his placidity even more marked than usual, stalked on into the parlor, where Mr. Blackstone, taking the chair *pro tem.*, read them the preliminary agreement he had drawn up; upon which Sam Turner immediately started to wrangle, a proceeding which proved altogether in vain.

The best he could get for patents and promotion was two thousand out of the five thousand shares of common stock, and finally he gave in, knowing that he could not secure the right kind of men on better terms. Mr. Blackstone thereupon offered a subscription list, to which every man present solemnly appended his name opposite the number of shares he would take. Sam, at the last moment, put down his own name for a block of stock which meant a cash investment of considerably more than he had originally figured upon. He cast up the list hurriedly. Five hundred shares of preferred, carrying half that much common, were still to be subscribed. With whom could he combine to obtain control? The only men who had subscribed enough for that purpose were Princeman, who was out of the question, and, in fact, would be the leader of the opposition, and Westlake. The highest of the others were Creamer, Cuthbert and Stevens. Sam would have to subscribe for the entire five hundred in order to make these men available to him.

McComas and Blackstone had only subscribed for the same amount as Sam. They could do him no good, and he knew it was hopeless to attempt to get two men to join with him. He looked over at Westlake. That gentleman was smiling like a placid cherub, all innocence without, and kindliness and good deeds; but there was nevertheless something fishy about Westlake's eyes, and Sam, in memory, cast over a list of maimed and wounded and crushed who had come in Westlake's business way. The logical candidate was Stevens. Stevens simply had to take enough stock to overbalance this thing, then he simply must vote his stock with Sam's! That was all there was to it! Sam did not pause to worry about how he was to gain over Stevens' consent, but he had an intuitive feeling that this was his only chance.

"Stevens," said he briskly, "there are five hundred shares left. I'll take half of it if you'll take the other half."

His brother Jack looked at him startled. Their total holdings, in that case, would mean an investment of more money than they could spare from their other operations. It would cramp them tremendously, but Jack ventured no objections. He had seen Sam at the helm in decisive places too often to interfere with him, either by word or look. As a matter of fact such a proceeding was not safe anyhow.

"I don't mind—" began Westlake, slowly fixing a beaming eye upon Sam, and crossing his hands ponderously upon his periphery; but before he could announce his benevolent intention, Mr. Stevens, with what might almost have been considered a malevolent glance toward Mr. Westlake, spoke up.

"I'll accept your proposition," he said with a jerk of his beard as his jaws snapped. So Miss Westlake thought a great deal of Sam, eh? And old

Westlake knew it, eh? And he had already subscribed enough stock to throw Sam control, eh?

"Thanks," said Sam, and shot Mr. Stevens a look of gratitude as he altered the subscription figures.

"Stop just a moment, Sam," put in Mr. Westlake. "How many shares of common stock does that give you in combination with your bonus?"

"Two thousand two hundred and sixty," said Sam.

"Oh!" said Mr. Westlake musingly; "not enough for control by two hundred and forty one shares; so you won't mind, since you haven't enough for control anyhow, if I take up that additional two hundred and fifty shares of preferred, with its one hundred and twenty-five of common, myself."

Sam once more paused and glanced over the subscription list. As it stood now, aside from Princeman, there were two members, Westlake and Stevens, with whom, if he could get either one of them to do so, he could pool his common stock. If he allowed Westlake to take up this additional two hundred and fifty shares, Westlake was the only string to his bow.

"No, thanks," said Sam. "I prefer to keep them myself. It seems to me to be a very fair and equitable division just as it is."

In the end it stood just that way.

CHAPTER XV.
THE HERO OF THE HOUR

On that very same afternoon, the youth and beauty, also the age and wisdom, of both Hollis Creek and Meadow Brook, gathered around the ball field of the former resort, to watch the Titanic struggle for victory between the two picked nines. As Sam took his place behind the bat for the first man up, who was Hollis, he felt his first touch of self-confidence anent the strictly amusement features of summer resorting. In all the other athletic pursuits he had been backward, but here, as he smacked his fist in his glove, he felt at home.

The only thing he did not like about it, as Princeman wound himself up to deliver the first ball, was that Princeman had the position of glory. On that gentleman the spotlight burned brightly all the time, and if they won, he would be the hero of the hour; the modest, reliable catcher would scarcely be thought of except by the men who knew the finer points of the game, and it was not the men whom he had in mind. Honestly and sincerely, he desired to shine before Miss Josephine Stevens. She was over there at the edge of the field under an oak tree.

Before her, cavorting for her amusement, were not only Princeman and himself, but Billy Westlake and Hollis, each of them alert for action at this moment; for now Princeman, with a mighty twirl upon his great toe, released the ball. It never reached Sam Turner's hands; instead it bounced off the bat with a "crack!" and sailed right down through Billy Westlake, who, at second, made a frantic grab for it, and then it spun out between center and right field, losing itself in the bushes, while Hollis, amid the frantic cheers of the audience, which consisted of Miss Josephine Stevens and several unconsidered other spectators, tore around the circuit. His colleagues strove wildly to hold Hollis at third, for the ball was found and was sailing over to that base. It arrived there just as he did, but far over the head of the third baseman, and fat, curly-haired Hollis, who looked like an ice wagon but ran like a motorcycle, secured the first run for Hollis Creek.

The next batter was up. Princeman, his confidence loftily unshaken, gave a correct imitation of a pretzel and delivered the ball. The batsman swung viciously at it.

Spat! It landed in Sam's glove.

"Strike one!" called the strident voice of Blackrock, who, jerking himself back several years into youth again, was umpiring the game with great joy. Nonchalantly Sam snapped the ball back over-hand. Princeman smiled with calm superiority. He wound himself up.

Spat! The ball had cut the plate and was in Sam's hands, while the batsman stood looking earnestly at the path over which it had come.

"Strike two!" called Blackstone.

Sam jerked the ball back with an underwrist toss of great perfection. Princeman drew himself up with smiling ease and posed a moment for the edification of the on-lookers. Sam Turner was the very first to detect the unbearable arrogance of that pose. Princeman eyed the batsman critically, mercilessly even, and delivered the third fatal plate-splitter.

Z-z-z-ing! The sphere slammed right out through Billy Westlake, who made a frantic grab for it. It bounded down between center and right field, and the players bumped shoulders in trying to stop it. It nestled among the bushes. The batsman tore around the bases. His colleagues tried to hold him at third, for the ball was streaking in that direction, but the batsman pawed straight on. The ball crossed the base before he did, but it bounded between the third sacker's feet, and score two was marked up for Hollis Creek, with nobody out!

With undiminished confidence, though somewhat annoyed, Princeman made a cute little knot of himself for the next batsman.

Spat! The ball landed in Sam's glove, two feet wide of the plate.

"Ball one!" called Blackstone.

Spat! In Sam's glove again, with the batsman jumping back to save his ribs.

"Ball two!" cried Blackstone.

Spat!

"Ball three."

"Put 'em over, Princeman!" yelled Billy Westlake from second.

"Don't be afraid of him! He couldn't hit it with a pillow!" jeered the third baseman.

In a calm, superior sort of way, Mr. Princeman smiled and shot over the ball.

"Four balls. Take your base!" said Mr. Blackstone, quite gently.

Reassuringly Mr. Princeman smiled upon his supporters, consisting of Miss Josephine Stevens and some other summer resorters, and proceeded to take out his revenge upon the next batter. The first two lofts were declared to be balls, and then Sam, catching his man playing too far off, snapped the pill down to the nearest suburb and nailed the first out. Encouraged by this, Princeman put over three successive strikes, and there were two gone. The next batter up, however, laced out, for two easy way-points, the first ball presented him. The next athlete brought him in with a single, and the next one put down a three-bagger which bored straight through Princeman and short stop and center field. That inglorious inning ended with a brilliant throw of Sam's to Billy Westlake at second, nipping a would-be thief who had hoped to purloin the seventh tally for Hollis Creek.

Billy Westlake, then taking the bat, increased the Meadow Brook depression by slapping the soft summer air three vicious spanks and retiring to think it over, and young Tilloughby bounced a feeble little bunt square at the feet of Hollis and was tossed out at first by something like six furlongs. The third batsman popped up a slow, lazy foul which gave the catcher almost plenty of time to roll a cigarette before it came down, and the Meadow Brook side was ignominiously retired. Score, six to nothing at the end of the first.

Princeman hit the first man up in the next inning and sent him down to the initial bag, which was a flat stone, happily limping. He issued free transportation to the next man and let the cripple hobble on to second, chortling with glee. The third man went to the first station on a measly little bunt with which Sam and Princeman and third base did some neat and shifty foot work, and the next man up soaked out a Wright Brothers beauty among the trees over beyond left field, and cleared the bases amid the perfectly frantic rejoicing of the fickle Miss Josephine Stevens and all the negligible balance of Hollis Creek. Oh, it was disgraceful! Sam Turner ground his teeth in impotent rage. He walked up to Princeman.

"Say, old man," he pleaded. "We've just *got* to settle down! We *must* pull this game out of the fire! We *can't* let Hollis Creek walk away with it!"

Princeman was pale, but clutched at his fast-slipping-away nonchalance with the grip of desperation.

"We'll hold them," he declared, and with careful deliberation he put over a ball which the next batter sent sailing right down inside the right foul line, pulling the first baseman away back almost to right field. Princeman stood gaping at that bingle in paralyzed dismay; but the batsman, who was a slow runner and slow thinker, stood a fatal second to see whether the ball was fair or foul. Almost at the crack of the bat Sam Turner started, raced down to first, caught the right fielder's throw and stepped on the stone, one handsome stride ahead of the runner! Then, as Blackrock, speechless with admiration, waved the runner out, the first mighty howl went up from Meadow Brook, and one partisan of the Hollis Creek nine, turning her back for the moment squarely upon her own colors, led the cheering. Sam heard her voice. It was a solo, while all the rest of the cheering was a faint accompaniment, and with such elation as comes only to the heroes in victorious battle, he trotted back to his place and caught three balls and three strikes on the next batter. Also, the next one went out on a pop fly which Sam was able to catch.

In their half Princeman redeemed himself in part by a three bagger which brought in two scores, and the second inning ended at ten to three in favor of Hollis Creek.

Confident and smiling, reinforced by the memory of his three bagger, Princeman took the mount for the beginning of the third, and with his compliments he suavely and politely presented a base to the first man up. A groan arose from all Meadow Brook. The second batsman shot a stinger to Princeman, who dropped it, and that batsman immediately thereafter roosted on first, crowing triumphantly; but the hot liner allowed Princeman a graceful opportunity. He complained of a badly hurt finger on his pitching hand. He called time while he held that injured member, and expressed in violent gestures the intolerable agony of it. Bravely, however, he insisted upon "sticking it out," and passed two wild ones up to the next willow wielder; then, having proved his gameness, he nobly sacrificed himself for the good of Meadow Brook, called time and asked for a substitute pitcher. He would go anywhere. He would take the field or he would retire. What he wanted was Meadow Brook to win. This was precisely what Sam Turner also wanted, and he lost no time in calling, with ill-concealed satisfaction, upon his brother Jack. Then Jack Turner, nothing loath, deserted his comfortable seat by the side of Miss Josephine Stevens, and strode forth to the mound, leaving the unfortunate Princeman to take his place by the side of Miss Stevens and give her an opportunity to sympathize with his poor maimed pitching hand, which, after a perfunctory moment of interest, she was too busy to do; for Jack Turner and Sam Turner, smiling across at each other in mutual confidence and esteem, proceeded to strike out the next three batters in succession, leaving men cemented to first and second bases, where they had been wildly imploring for opportunities to tear themselves loose.

What need to tell of the balance of that game; of the calm, easy, one-two-three work of the invincible Turner battery; of the brilliant base throwing and fielding of Turner and Turner, and their mighty swats when they came to bat? You know how the game turned out. Anybody would know. It ended in a triumph for Meadow Brook at the end of the seventh inning, which is all any summer resort game ever goes, and two innings more than most, by a total and glorious score of twenty-one to seventeen. And who were the heroes of the hour, as smilingly but modestly they strode from the diamond? Who, indeed, but Jack Turner and Sam Turner; and by token of their victory, after receiving the frenzied plaudits of all Meadow Brook and the generous plaudits of all Hollis Creek, they marched in triumph from the field, one on either side of Miss Josephine Stevens! Where now were Hollis and Princeman and Billy Westlake? Nowhere! They were forgotten of men, ignored of women, and the laurels of sweet victory rested upon the brow of busy Sam Turner!

CHAPTER XVI.
AN INTERRUPTED BUT PROPERLY FINISHED
PROPOSAL OF MARRIAGE

Jack's first opportunity for a quiet talk with his brother did not occur for an hour after the game.

"I don't like to worry you while you're resting, Sam," he began, "but I'll have to tell you that the Flatbush deal seems likely to drop through. It reaches a head to-morrow, you know."

Sam Turner grabbed for his watch.

"It can't drop through!" he vigorously declared. "I'll go right up there to-night and look after it."

"But you're on your vacation," protested Jack. "That's no way to rest."

"On my vacation!" snorted Sam. "Of course I am. I'm not losing a minute of my vacation. The proper way to have a vacation is to do the thing you enjoy most. Don't you suppose I'll enjoy closing that Flatbush deal?"

"Certainly," admitted his brother, "and I'll enjoy seeing you do it. I know you can."

"Of course I can. But you're to stay here."

"It's not my turn for an outing," protested Jack. "I haven't earned one yet."

"You're to work," explained Sam. "You see, Jack, in one week I can't become a bowling or golf expert enough to beat Princeman, nor a tennis or dancing expert enough to outshine Billy Westlake, nor a horseback or croquet expert enough to make a deuce out of Hollis. You can do all these things, and I want you to give this crowd of distinguished amateurs a showing up. Jack, if you ever worked for athletic honors in your life now is the time to do it; and in between time stick to Miss Stevens like glue. Monopolize her. Don't give these three or any other contenders any of her time. Keep her busy. Let me know every day what progress you're making; don't stop to write; wire! For remember, Jack, I'm going to marry her. I've got to."

"Well, then you'll marry her," Jack sagely concluded. "Does she know it yet?"

"I don't think she's quite sure of it," returned Sam with careful analysis. "Of course she's thought about it. Sometimes she thinks she won't, and sometimes she thinks she will, and sometimes she isn't quite sure whether she will or not. Don't you worry about that part, though, and don't bother to boost me. Just quietly you take the shine out of these summer champions and leave the rest to your brother Sam."

"Fine," agreed Jack. "Run right along and sell your papers, Sammy, and I'll wire you every time I put over a point."

Sam hunted and found Miss Josephine.

"I'm sorry I have to take a run back to New York for two or three days," he said.

She bent upon him a glance of amusement; the old glance of mingled amusement and mischief.

"I thought you were on your vacation," she observed.

"And I am," he insisted. "I've been having a bully time, and I'll come back here to finish up the couple of days I have left."

"Then the drive which didn't count this morning, and which was postponed again until to-morrow morning, will have to be put off once more," she reminded him with a gay laugh.

"By George, that's so!" he exclaimed. "In all the excitement it had quite slipped my mind."

"I presume you're going up on business," she slyly observed.

"Yes, I am," he admitted.

She laughed and gave him her hand.

"Well, I wish you good luck," she said. "I hope you make all the money in the world. But you won't forget us who are down here in the country dawdling away our time in useless amusements."

"Forget you!" he returned impetuously. "Never for a minute!" and he was in such deadly earnest about it that she hastily checked further speech, although she did not know why.

"Good!" she hurriedly exclaimed. "I'm glad you will bear us in mind while you're gone. Are you going to take your brother along?"

"No," he said with a smile. "I'm putting him in as my vacation substitute, and I'll give him special instructions to call you up every morning for orders. You'll find him in perfect discipline. He'll do whatever you tell him."

"I shall give him a thorough trial," she laughed. "I never yet had anybody to come and go abjectly at the word of command, and I think it will be a delightful novelty."

Jack approaching just then, she took his arm quite comfortably.

"Your brother tells me that during his absence you are to be my chief aide and attaché," she advised that young man gaily; "that you'll fetch and carry and do what I tell you; and the first thing you must do is to call for me when you take Mr. Turner to the train."

It is glorious to part so pleasantly as that from people you have persistently in mind, and Sam, with such cheerful recollections, enjoyed his vacation to the full as he did new and brilliant and unexpected things in closing up the Flatbush deal, keeping, in the meantime, in constant touch with his office and with such telegrams as these:

"Established new tennis record this morning Westlake nowhere and has been snubbed do not know why."

"Bowled two eighty five last night against Princeman two twenty am teaching her."

"Danced six dances out of twelve with her says I'm better dancer than Billy Westlake."

"Jumped Hollis Creek after her hat on horseback this afternoon Hollis dared not follow am to give her riding lessons."

Then came this one:

"Her father just told me she refused Princeman last night she will not talk to Hollis and scarcely to me is dull and does not eat I beat all entries in ten mile Marathon today and she hardly applauded wire instructions."

Sam Turner took the next train. One look at Miss Stevens, after he had traveled two years to reach Restview, made him suddenly intoxicated, for in her eyes there was ravenous hunger for him and he read it, and feeling rather sure of his ground he determined that now was the time to strike. With that decisive end in view he dropped Jack at Meadow Brook and went right on over to Hollis Creek with Miss Josephine. Of course there was no chance to talk quite intimately, with Henry up there ahead listening with all his ears, but there was every chance in the world to look into her eyes and grow delirious; to touch elbows; to look again and gaze deep into her eyes and see her turn away startled and half frightened; to say perfunctory things which meant nothing and everything, and receive perfunctory answers which meant as little and as much; but before they had arrived at Hollis Creek Sam was frankly and boldly holding her hand and she was letting him do it, and they were both of them profoundly happy and profoundly silly, and would just as leave have ridden on that way for ever.

Words seemed superfluous, but yet they were more or less necessary, so Sam got out at Hollis Creek Inn with her, and led the way determinedly and directly into the stuffy little parlor just off the main assembly room. He saw Mr. Stevens in the door of the post-office, but only nodded to him, and then he drew Miss Josephine into the corner freest from observation.

"You know why I came back," he informed her, fixing her with a masterly eye; "I had to see you again. My whole life is changed since I met you. I need you. I can not do without you. I—"

"Beg your pardon, Sam," said Mr. Stevens, appearing suddenly in the doorway, and then he paused, much more confused even than the young people, for Sam was holding both Miss Josephine's hands and gazing down at her with an earnestness which, if harnessed, would have driven a four-ton dynamo; and she was gazing up at him just as earnestly, with an entirely breathless, but by no means displeased expression.

"Excuse me!" stammered Mr. Stevens.

It was Miss Josephine who first found her aplomb. She smiled her rare smile of mingled amusement and mischief at Sam, and then at her father.

"You're quite excusable, I guess, father," she said sweetly. "What is it?"

"Why, your brother Jack just called you up from Meadow Brook, Sam, and wants to tell you something immediately," stammered Mr. Stevens, plucking at a beard which in that moment seemed to have lost all its aggressiveness. "He called twice before you arrived, and is on the 'phone now."

Sam, as he walked to the telephone, had time to find that his heart was beating a tattoo against his ribs, that his breath was short and fluttery, and that stage fright had suddenly crept over him and claimed him for its own; so it was with no great patience or understanding that he heard Jack tell him in great glee about some tests which Princeman had had made in his own paper mills with the marsh pulp, and how Princeman was sorry he had not taken more stock, and could not the treasury stock be opened for further subscription? "Tell him no," said Sam shortly, and hung up the receiver; then he repented of his bluntness and spent five precious minutes in recalling his brother and apologizing for his bruskness, explaining that Princeman was probably trying to plan another attempt to pool the stock.

In the meantime Theophilus Stevens had stood surveying his daughter in contrition.

"I'm afraid I came in at a most inopportune moment," he said by way of apology.

"Yes, I'm afraid you did," she admitted with a smile. "However, I don't think Sam will forget what he wanted to say," and suddenly she reached up and put her arms around her father's neck and drew his face down and kissed him rapturously.

"I'm glad to see you feel the way you do about it," said Mr. Stevens delightedly, petting her gently upon the shoulder with one hand and with the other smoothing back the hair from her forehead. She was the dearest to him of all his children, although he never confessed it, even to himself, and just now they were very, very close together indeed. "I'm glad to hear you call him Sam, too. He's a fine young man and he is bound to be a howling success in everything he undertakes." He smiled reminiscently. "I rather thought there was something between you two," he went on, still patting her shoulder, "and when Dan Westlake told me that his girl thought a great deal of Sam and that he was going to buy enough stock in Sam's company to give Sam control, I turned right around and bought just as much stock as Westlake had, although just before the meeting I had refused to invest as much money as Sam wanted me to. Moreover, Westlake and myself, between us, stopped the move to pool the outside stock, just yet. He's a smart young man, that boy," he continued admiringly. "I didn't see, until I went into that meeting, why he was so crazy to have me buy enough stock to gain control— What's the matter?"

He stopped in perplexity, for his daughter, looking aghast at him, had pushed back from his embrace and was regarding him with perfectly round eyes, while over her face, at first pale, there gradually crept a crimson flush.

"Well, of all things!" she gasped. "Of all the cold-blooded, cruel, barter-and-sale proceedings! Why, father, how—how could you! How could he! I never in all my life—"

"Why, Jo, what do you mean? What's the trouble?"

"If you don't understand I can't make you," she said helplessly.

"Well, I'll be—busted!" observed Mr. Stevens under his breath.

To his infinite relief Sam came in just then, and Mr. Stevens, wondering what he had done now, slipped hastily out of the room. Mr. Turner, coming from the bright office into the dim room and innocent of any change in the atmosphere, approached confidently and eagerly to Miss Josephine with both hands extended, but she stepped back most indignantly.

"You need not finish what you were going to say!" she warned him. "My father has just given me some information which changes the entire aspect of affairs. I am not a part of a business bargain! I refuse to be regarded as a commercial proposition! I heard something from Mr. Princeman of what desperate efforts you were making to secure the command, whatever that may be, of the—of the stock—board—of shares in your new company, but I did not think you would go to such lengths as this!"

"Why, my dear girl," began Sam, shocked.

"I am not your dear girl and I never shall be," she told him, and angrily dabbed at some sudden tears. "I never was. I was only a business possibility."

"That's unjust," he charged her. "I don't see how you could accuse me of regarding you in any other way than as the dearest and the sweetest and the most beautiful girl in all the world, the wisest and the most sensible, the most faithful, the most charming, the most delightful, the most everything that is desirable."

"Wait just a moment," she told him, very coldly indeed; with almost extravagant coldness, in fact, as she beat out of her consciousness the enticing epithets he had bestowed upon her. "Do you mean to say that never in your calculations did you consider that if you married me my father would vote his stock with yours—I believe that's the way he puts it—and give you command or whatever it is of your company?"

"Well," considered Sam, brought to a standstill and put straight upon his honor, "I can't deny that it did seem to me a very satisfactory thing that my father-in-law should own enough stock in the company—"

"That will do," she interrupted him icily. "That is precisely what I have charged. We will consider this subject as ended, Mr. Turner; as one never to be referred to again."

"We'll do nothing of the sort," returned Sam flat-footedly. "I've been composing this speech for the last two weeks and I'm going to deliver it. I'm not going to have it wasted. I've unconsciously been rehearsing it every place I went. Even up in Flatbush, showing a man the superior advantages of that yellow-mud district, I found myself repeating sentence number twelve. It's been the first thing I thought of in the morning and the last thing I thought of at night. It's been with me all day, riding and walking and talking and eating and drinking and just breathing. Now I'm going to go through with it.

"I—I—confound it all! I've forgotten how I was going to say it now! After all, though, it only amounted to this: I love you! I want you to know it and understand it. I love you and love you and love you! I never loved any woman before in my life. I never had time. I didn't know what it was like. If I had I'd have fought it off until I met you, because I could not afford it for anybody short of you. It takes my whole attention. It distracts my mind entirely from other things. I can't think of anything else consecutively and connectedly. I—I'm sorry you take the attitude you do about this thing, but—I'm not going to accept your viewpoint. You've got to look at this thing differently to understand it.

"I know you've been glad I loved you. You were glad the first day we met, and you always will be glad! Whatever you have to say about it just now don't count. I'm going to let you alone a while to think it over, and then I'm coming back to tell you more about it," and with that Sam stalked from the room, leaving Miss Josephine Stevens gasping, dazed, quite sure that he was unforgivable, indignant with everything, still rankling, in spite of all Sam had said, with the thought that she had been made a mere part of a commercial transaction. Why, it was like those barbarous countries she had read about, where wives are bought and sold! Preposterous and unbearable!

While she was in this storm of mixed emotions her father came in upon her, this time seriously perplexed.

"What has happened to Sam Turner?" he demanded. "He slammed out of the house, passed me on the porch with only a grunt, and jumped into his automobile. You must have done something to anger him."

"I hope that I did!" she retorted with spirit. "I refused to marry him."

"You did!" he returned in surprise. "Why, I thought it was all cut and dried between you."

"It was until you blundered into us and spoiled everything," she charged. "But I'm glad you did. You let me know that Sam Turner wanted to marry me because you had bought shares enough in his company to give him the advantage. I'm ashamed of you and ashamed of Sam—of Mr. Turner—and ashamed of myself. Why, you make a bargain-counter remnant of me! I never, *never* was so humiliated!"

"Poor child!" her father blandly sympathized. "Also, poor Sam. By the way, though, he doesn't need you to secure control of his company. Dan Westlake, as I told you, has bought enough stock to do the work, and Miss Westlake would marry him in a minute. If Sam wants control of his company, he only has to go to her and say the word."

"Father!" exclaimed his daughter with stern indignation. "I don't see how you can even suggest that!"

"Suggest what? Now, what have I said?"

"That Sam—that Mr. Turner would even dream of marrying that Westlake girl, just in order to get the better of a business transaction," and very much to Theophilus Stevens' surprise and consternation and dismay, she suddenly crumpled up in a heap in her chair and burst out crying.

"Well, I'll be busted!" her father muttered into his beard.

CHAPTER XVII.
SHE CALLS HIM SAM!

Miss Josephine, finding all ordinary occupations stale, unprofitable and wearisome on the following morning, and finding herself, moreover, possessed of a restless spirit which urged her to do something or other and yet recoiled at each suggestion she made it, started out quite aimlessly to walk by herself. She walked in the direction of Meadow Brook. The paths in that direction were so much prettier.

Sam Turner, finding all other occupations stale, unprofitable and wearisome, at the same moment started out to walk by himself, going in the direction of Hollis Creek because that was the exact direction in which he wanted to go. As he walked much more rapidly than Miss Stevens, he arrived midway of the distance before she did, but at the valley where the unnamed stream came rippling down he paused.

He had looked often at this little hollow as he had passed it, and every time he had looked upon it he seemed to have an idea of some sort in the back of his head regarding it; a dim, unformed, fugitive sort of idea which had never asserted itself very prominently because he had been too busy to listen to its rather timid voice.

Just now, however, the idea suddenly struggled to make itself loudly known, whereupon Sam bade it come forth. Given hearing it proved to be a very pleasant idea, and a forceful one as well; so much so that it even checked the speed with which Sam had set out for Hollis Creek. He looked calculatingly across the road to where the little stream went flashing from under its wooden bridge across the field and hid around a curve behind some bushes, then reappeared, dancing in the sunlight, until finally it plunged among some far trees and was lost to him. He gazed up the stream. He had not very far to look, for there it ran down between two quite steep hills, through a sort of pocket valley, closed or almost closed, at the upper end, by another hill equally steep, its waters being augmented by a leaping little stream from a strong spring hidden away somewhere in the hill to the left.

As his eyes calculatingly swept stream and hills, they suddenly caught a flutter of white through the trees, and it was coming down the winding path which led across the hills to Hollis Creek. As it emerged more from the concealment of the leaves his blood gave a leap, for the flutter of white was a gown inclosing the unmistakable figure of Miss Josephine Stevens. The whole valley suddenly seemed radiant.

"Hello!" he called to her as she approached. "I didn't expect to find you here."

"I did not expect to be here," she laughed. "I just started out for a stroll and happened to land in this beautiful spot."

"Beautiful is no name for it," he replied with sudden vast enthusiasm, and ran up the path to help her down over a steep place.

For a moment, in the wonderful mystery of the touch of her hand and the joy of her presence, he forgot everything else. What was this strange phenomenon, by which the mere presence of one particular person filled all the air with a tingling glow? Marvelous, that's what it was! If Miss Josephine had any of the same wonder she was extremely careful not to express it, nor let it show, especially after yesterday's conversation, so she immediately talked of other things; and the first thing which came handy was another reference to the beautiful valley.

"You know, it is a wonder to me," she said, "that no one has built a summer resort here. I think it ever so much more charming than either Hollis Creek or Meadow Brook."

"Do you believe in telepathy?" asked Sam, almost startled. "I do. It hasn't been but a few minutes since that identical idea popped into my head, and I had just now decided that if I could secure options on this property I would have a real summer resort here—one that would make Hollis Creek and Meadow Brook mere farm boarding-houses. Do you see how close together these hills draw at their feet? The hollow is at least a thousand feet across at the widest part, but down there at the road, where the stream emerges to the fields, they close in with natural buttresses, as it were, to not over a hundred feet in width. Well, right across there we'll build a dam, and there is enough water here to make a beautiful lake up as high as that yellow rock."

Miss Josephine looked up at the yellow rock and clasped her hands with an exclamation of delight.

"Glorious!" she said. "I never would have thought of that; and how beautiful it will be! Why, if the lake comes up that high it will go clear back around that turn in the valley, won't it?"

"Easily," he replied; "although that might make us trouble, for I don't know where that turn in the valley leads. I have never explored that region. Suppose we go up and look it over."

"Won't that be fun?" she agreed, and they started to follow the stream.

As they reached the rear of the "pocket," where they could see around the curve, they turned and looked back over the route they had just traversed.

"My idea," Sam explained, having waited until they reached this viewpoint to do so, "is to build the dam down there at the roadside, and build the hotel right over it so that arriving guests will, after an elevator has brought them up to the height of the main floor, find the blue of the lake suddenly bursting upon them from the main piazza, which will face the valley. All of the inside rooms will, of course, have hanging balconies looking out over the water."

"Perfectly ideal!" she agreed, her enthusiasm growing.

"I think I'd better investigate the curve of the valley," he decided, studying the path carefully. "It seems rather rough for you, and I'll go alone. All I want to see is how far the water height will carry around there, and if it will become necessary to build a dam at the other end."

"Oh, it isn't too rough for me," she declared immediately. "I am an excellent climber," and together they started to explore the now narrowing valley, following the stream over steep rocks and fallen trees, and pushing through tangled undergrowth and among briers and bushes and around slippery banks until they came to another tortuous turn, where a second spring, welling up from under a flat, overhanging rock, tumbled down to augment the supply for the future lake; and here they stopped and had a drink of the cool, delicious water, Sam making the girl a cup from a huge leaf which she said made the water taste fuzzy, and then showing her how to get down on her hands and knees—spreading his coat on the ground to protect her gown—and drink *au naturel*, a trick at which she was most charming, and probably knew it.

The valley here had grown most narrow, but they followed the now very small stream around one sharp curve after another until they found its source, which was still another spring, and here there was no more valley; but a cleft in the hill to the right, which they suddenly came upon, gave them an exquisite view out over the beautiful low-lying country, miles in extent, which lay between this and the next range of hills; a delightful vista dotted with green farms and white farm-houses and smiling streams and waving trees and grazing cattle. They stopped in awe at the beauty of it and looked out over the valley in silence; and unconsciously the girl slipped her hand within the arm of the man!

"Just imagine a sunset out over there," he said. "You see those fleecy clouds that are out there now. If clouds like those are still there when the sun goes down, they will be a fleet of pearl-gray vessels, with carmine keels, upon a sea of gold."

She glanced at him quickly, but she did not express her marvel that this man had so many sides. Before she could comment, and while she was still framing some way to express her appreciation of his gentler gifts, he returned briskly to practical things.

"Our lake will scarcely come up to this point," he judged. "I don't think that at any point it will be high enough to cover the springs. We don't want it to if we can help it, for that would destroy some of the beauty of it. Have you noticed that our lake will be much like a kite in shape, with this winding ravine the tail of it. We'll have to take in a lot of acreage to cover this property, but it will be worth it. I'm going to look after options right away. I'm glad now I had already decided to stay another two weeks."

Of course she was still angry with Sam, she reminded herself, but she was inexpressibly glad, somehow or other, to find that he was intending to stay two weeks longer, and was startled as she recognized that fact.

"It will take a lot of money, won't it, to build a hotel here?" she asked, getting away from certain troublesome thoughts as quickly as she could.

"Yes, it will take a great deal," he admitted, as they turned to scramble down the ravine again. "I should judge, however, that about two hundred and fifty thousand dollars would finance it."

"But I thought, from something father once said, that you did not have so much money as that?"

"Bless you, no!" replied Sam, smiling. "No indeed! I've enough to cover an option on this property and that's about all, now, since I'm tangled up so deeply with my Pulp Company, but I figure that I can make a quick turn on this property to help me out on the other thing. What I'll do," he explained, "is to get this option first of all, and then have some plans drawn, including a nice perspective view of the hotel—a water-color sketch, you know, showing the building fronting the lake—and upon that build a prospectus to get up the stock company. I'll take stock for my control of the land and for my services in promotion. Then I'll sell my stock and get out. I ought to make the turn in two or three months and come out fifteen, or possibly twenty or twenty-five thousand dollars to the good. It is a nice, big scheme."

"Oh," she said blankly, "then you wouldn't actually build a hotel yourself?"

"Hardly," he returned. "I'll be content to make the profit out of promoting it that I'd make in the first four or five years of running the place."

"I see," she said musingly; "and you'd get this up just like you formed your Marsh Pulp Company, I think father called it, and of course you'd try to get—what is it?—oh, yes; control."

He smiled at her.

"I'd scarcely look for that in this deal," he explained. "If I can just get a nice slice of promotion stock and sell it I shall be quite well satisfied."

She bent puzzled brows over this new problem.

"I don't quite understand how you can do it," she confessed, "but of course you know how. You're used to these things. Father says you're very good at promoting."

"That's the way I've made all my money, or rather what little I have," he told her, modestly enough. "I expect this Pulp Company, however, to lift me out of that, for a few years at least; then when I come back into the promoting field I can go after things on a big scale. The Pulp Company ought to make me a lot of money if I can just keep it in my own hands," and involuntarily he sighed.

She looked at him musingly for a moment, and was about to say something, but thought better of it and said something else.

"The tail of your kite will be almost a perfect letter 'S'," she observed. "How beautiful it will be; the big, broad lake out there in the main valley, and then the nice, little, secluded, twisty waterway back in through here; a regular lover's lane of a waterway, as it were. I don't suppose these springs have any names. They must be named, and—why, we haven't even named the lake!"

"Yes, we have," he quickly returned. "I'm going to call it Lake Josephine."

"You haven't asked my permission for that," she objected with mock severity.

"There are plenty of Josephines in the world," he calmly observed. "Nobody has a copyright on the name, you know."

She smiled, as one sure of her ground.

"Yes, but you wouldn't call it that, if I were to object seriously."

"No, I guess I wouldn't," he gave up; "but you're not going to object seriously, are you?"

"I'll think it over," she said.

They were now making their way along a bank that was too difficult of travel to allow much conversation, though it did allow some delicious helping, but when they came out into the main valley where they could again look down on the road, they paused to survey the course over which they had just come, and to appreciate to the full the beauty of Sam's plan.

"I don't believe I quite like your idea of the hotel built down there at the roadside," she objected as they sat on a huge boulder to rest. "It cuts off the view of the lake from passers-by, and I should think it would be the best advertisement you could have for everybody who drove past there to say: 'Oh, what a pretty place!' Now I should think that right about here where we are sitting would be the proper location for your hotel. Just think how the lake and the building would look from the road. Right here would be a broad porch jutting out over the water, giving a view down that first bend of the kite tail, and back of the hotel would be this big hill and all the trees, and hills and trees would spread out each side of it, sort of open armed, as it were, welcoming people in."

"It couldn't be seen, though," objected Sam. "The dam down there would necessarily be about thirty feet high at the center, and people driving along the roadway would not be able to see the water at all. They would only see the blank wall of the dam. Of course we could soften that by building the dam back a few feet from the roadway, making an embankment and covering that with turf, or possibly shrubbery or flowers, but still the water would not be visible, nor the hotel!"

"I see," she said slowly.

They both studied that objection in silence for quite a little while. Then she suddenly and excitedly ejaculated:

"*Sam!*"

He jumped, and he thrilled all through. She had called him Sam entirely unconsciously, which showed that she had been thinking of him by that familiar name. With the exclamation had come sparkling eyes and heightened color, not due to having used the word, but due to a bright thought, and he almost lost his sense of logic in considering the delightful combination. It occurred to him, however, that it would be very unwise for him to call attention to her slip of the tongue, or even to give her time to think and recognize it herself.

"Another idea?" he asked.

"Indeed yes," she asserted, "and this time I know it's feasible. I don't know much about measurements in feet and inches, but there are three feet in a yard."

"Yes."

"Well, doesn't the road down there, from hill to hill, dip about ten yards?"

"Yes."

"Well then, that's thirty feet, just as high as you say the dam will have to be. Why not raise the road itself thirty feet, letting it be level and just as high as your dam?"

Sam rose and solemnly shook hands with her.

"You must come into the firm," he declared. "That solves the entire problem. We'll run a culvert underneath there to the fields. The road will reinforce the dam and the edge of the dam will be entirely concealed. It will be merely a retaining wall with a nice stone coping, which will be repeated on the field side. There will be no objection from the county commissioners, because we shall improve the road by taking two steep hills out of it. Your plan is much better than mine. I can see myself, for instance, driving along that road on my way to Hollis Creek from Restview, looking over that beautiful little lake to the hotel beyond, and saying to myself: 'Well, next summer I won't stop at Hollis Creek. I'll stop at Lake Jo.'"

"I thought it was to be Lake Josephine," she interposed.

"I thought so too," he agreed, "but Lake Jo just slipped out. It seems so much better. Lake Jo! That would look fine on a prospectus."

"You'd print the cover of it in blue and gold, I suppose, wouldn't you?"

"There would need to be a splash of brown-red in it," he reminded her, considering color schemes for a moment. "The roof of the hotel would, of course, be red tile. We'd build it fireproof. There is plenty of gray stone around here, and we'd build it of native rock."

"And then," she went on, in the full swing of their idea, "think of the beautiful walks and climbs you could have among these hills; and the driveway! Your approach to the hotel would come around the dam and up that hill, would wind up through those trees and rocks, and right here at the bend of the ravine it would cross the thick part of the kite tail to the hotel on a quaint rustic bridge; and as people arrived and departed you'd hear the clatter of the horses' hoofs."

"Great!" he exclaimed, catching her enthusiasm and with it augmenting his own, "and guests leaving would first wave good-by at the porte-cochère just about where we are sitting. They'd clatter across the bridge, with their friends on the porch still fluttering handkerchiefs after them; they'd disappear into the trees over yonder and around through that cleft in the rocks. And see; on the other side of the cleft there is a little tableland which juts out, and the road would wind over that, where carriages would once more be seen from the hotel porch. Then they'd twist in through the trees again down the winding driveway, and once more, for the very last glimpse, come into view as they went across our new road in front of the lake; and there the last flutter of handkerchiefs would be seen. You know it's silly to stand and wave your friends out of sight for a long distance when they're always in view, but if the view is interrupted two or three times it relieves the monotony."

CHAPTER XVIII.
SAM TURNER ACQUIRES A BUSINESS PARTNER

They followed the stream down to the road, at every step gaging with the eye the height of the lake and judging the altered scenic view from the level of the water. There would be room for dozens and dozens of boats upon that surface without interference. Sam calculated that from the upper spring there would be headway enough to run a small fountain in the center, surrounded by a pond-lily bed which would be kept in place by a stone curbing. In the hill to the right there was a deep indenture. Back in there would go the bathing pavilions. They even went up to look at it, and were delighted to find a natural, shallow bowl. By cementing the floor of that bowl they could have a splendid swimming-pool for timid bathers, where they could not go beyond their depth; and it was entirely surrounded by a thick screen of shrubbery. Oh, it was delightful; it was perfect! At the road they looked back up over the valley again. It was no longer a valley. It was a lake. They could see the water there. Sam drew from his pocket a pencil and an envelope.

"The hotel will have to be long and tall," he observed, "for there will not be much room on that ledge, from front to back. The building will stretch out quite a ways. Three or four hundred feet long it will be, and about five stories in height," and taking a letter from the envelope, he sat down upon a fallen log and began rapidly to sketch.

He drew the hotel with wide-spreading Spanish roofs and balconies, and a wide porch with rippling water in front of it, and rowboats and people in them; and behind the hotel rose the broken sky-line of the hills and the trees, with an indication of fleecy clouds above. It was just a light sketch, a sort of shorthand picture, as it were, and yet it seemed full of sunlight and of atmosphere.

"I hadn't any idea you could draw like that," she exclaimed in admiration.

"I do a little of everything, I think, but nothing perfectly," he admitted with some regret.

"It seems to me you do everything excellently," she objected quite seriously; and she was, in fact, deeply impressed.

He walked over to the stream, a trifle confused, but not displeased, by any means, by the earnestness of her compliment.

"I must have the water analyzed to see if it has any medicinal virtue," he said. "The spring out of which we drank has a sweetish-like taste, but the water here—" and he caught up some of it in his hand and tasted it, "seems to be slightly salt."

He had left her sitting on the log with the sketch in her lap. Now the sketch fluttered to the ground and the letter turned over, right side up. It was a letter which Sam had written to his brother Jack and had not mailed because he had suddenly decided to come down to the scene of action. As she stooped over to pick it up her eyes caught the sentence: "I love her, Jack, more than I can tell you, more than I can tell anybody, more than I can tell myself. It's the most important, the most stupendous thing—" She hastily turned that letter over and was very careful to have it lying upon her lap, back upward, exactly as he had left it there, and when he came back she was very, very careful indeed to hand it nonchalantly over to him, with the sketch uppermost.

"Of course," he said, looking around him comprehensively, "this is only a day-dream, so far. It may be impossible to realize it."

"Why?" she asked, instantly concerned. "This project *must* be carried through! It is already as good as completed. It just must be done. I never before had a hand, even in a remote way, in planning a big thing, and I couldn't bear not to see this done. What is to prevent it?"

"I may not be able to get the land," returned Sam soberly. "It is probably owned by half a dozen people, and one or more of them is certain to want exorbitant prices for it."

"It certainly can't be very valuable," she protested. "It isn't fit for anything, is it?"

"For nothing but the building of Lake Jo," he agreed. "Right now it is worthless, but the minute anybody found out I wanted it it would become extremely valuable. The only way to do would be to see everybody at once and close the options before they could get to talking it over among themselves."

"What time is it?" she demanded.

He looked at his watch.

"Ten-thirty," he said.

"Then let's go and see all these people right away," she urged, jumping to her feet.

He smiled at her enthusiasm, but he was none loath to accept her suggestion.

"All right," he agreed. "I wish they had telephones here in the woods. We'll simply have to walk over to Meadow Brook and get an auto."

"Come on," she said energetically, and they started out on the road. They had not gone far, however, when young Tilloughby, with Miss Westlake, overtook them in a trap. He reined up, and Miss Westlake greeted the pedestrians with frigid courtesy. Jack Turner had accidentally dropped her a hint. Now that she had begun to appreciate Mr. Tilloughby—Bob—at his true value, she wondered what she had ever seen in Sam Turner—and she never had liked Josephine Stevens!

"Gug-gug-gug-glorious day, isn't it?" observed Tilloughby, his face glowing with joy.

"Fine," agreed Sam with enthusiasm. "There never was a more glorious day in all the world. You've just come along in time to save our lives, Tilloughby. Which way are you bound?"

"Wuw-wuw-wuw-we had intended to go around Bald Hill."

"Well, postpone that for a few minutes, won't you, Tilloughby, like a good fellow? Trot back to Meadow Brook and send an auto out here for us. Get Henry, by all means, to drive it."

"Wuw-wuw-wuw-with pleasure," replied Tilloughby, wondering at this strange whim, but restraining his curiosity like a thoroughbred. "Huh-huh-huh-Henry shall be back here for you in a jiffy," and he drove off in a cloud of dust.

Miss Stevens surveyed the retiring trap in satisfaction.

"Good," she exclaimed. "I already feel as though we were doing something to save Lake Jo."

They walked back quite contentedly to the valley and surveyed it anew, there resting now on both of them a sense of almost prideful possession. They discovered a high point on which a rustic observatory could be built; they planned paths and trails; they found where the water-line came just under an overhanging rock which would make a cave large enough for three or four boats to scurry under out of the rain. They found delightful surprises all along the bank of the future lake, and Miss Stevens declared that when the dam was built and the lake began to fill, she never intended to leave it except for meals, until it was up to the level at which they would permit the overflow to be opened.

Henry, returning with the automobile, found them far up in the valley discussing a floating band pavilion, but they came down quickly enough when they saw him, and scrambled into the tonneau with the haste of small children. Henry watched them take their places with smiling affection. He had not only had good tips but pleasant words from Sam, and Miss Stevens was her own incentive to good wishes and good will.

"Henry," said Sam, "we want to drive around to see the people who own this land."

"Oh, shucks," said Henry, disappointed. "I can't drive you there. The man that owns all this land lives in New York."

"In New York!" repeated Sam in dismay. "What would anybody in New York want with this?"

"The fellow that bought it got it about ten years ago," Henry informed them. "He was going to build a big country house, back up there in the hills, I understand, and raise deer to shoot at, and things like that; got an architect to make him plans for house and stables and all costing hundreds of thousands of dollars; but before he could break ground on it him and his wife had a spat and got a divorce. He tried to sell the land back again to the people he bought it from, but they wouldn't take it at any price. They were glad to be shut of it and none of his rich friends wanted to buy it after that, because, they said, there were so many of those cheap summer resorts around here."

"I see," said Sam musingly. "You don't happen to know the man's name, do you?"

"Dickson, I think it was. Henry Dickson. I remember his first name because it was the same as mine."

"Great!" exclaimed Sam, overjoyed. "Why, I know Henry Dickson like a book. I've engineered several deals for him. He's a mighty good friend of mine too. That simplifies matters. Drive us right over to Hollis Creek."

"To Hollis Creek!" she objected. "I should think you'd drive to Meadow Brook instead and dress for the trip. Aren't you going to catch that afternoon train and go right up there?"

"By no means. This is Saturday, and by the time I'd get to New York he couldn't be found anywhere; and anyhow, I wouldn't have time to deliver you at Hollis Creek and make this next train."

"Don't mind about me," she urged. "I could go to the train with you and Henry could take me back to Hollis Creek."

"That's fine of you," returned Sam gratefully; "but it isn't the program at all. I happen to know that Dickson stays in his office until one o'clock on Saturdays. I'll get him by long distance."

They were quite silent in calculation on the way to Hollis Creek, and Miss Josephine found herself pushing forward to help make the machine go faster. Breathlessly she followed Sam into the house, and he obligingly left the door of the telephone booth ajar, so that she could hear his conversation with Dickson.

"Hello, Dickson," said Sam, when he got his connection. "This is Sam Turner.... Oh yes, fine. Never better in my life.... Up here in Hamster County, taking a little vacation. Say, Dickson, I understand you own a thousand acres down here. Do you want to sell it?... How much?" As he received the answer to that question he turned to Miss Josephine and winked, while an expression of profound joy, albeit materialized into a grin, overspread his features. "I won't dicker with you on that price," he said into the telephone. "But will you take my note for it at six per cent.?"

He laughed aloud at the next reply.

"No, I don't want it to run that long. The interest in a hundred years would amount to too much; but I'll make it five years.... All right, Dickson, instruct your lawyer chap to make out the papers and I'll be up Monday to close with you."

He hung up the receiver and turned to meet her glistening eyes fixed upon him in ecstasy. "It's better than all right," he assured her. He was more enthusiastic about this than he had ever been about any business deal in his life, that is, more openly enthusiastic, for Miss Josephine's enthusiasm was contagion itself. He took her arm with a swing, and they hurried into the writing-room, which was deserted for the time being on account of the mail having just come in. Sam placed a chair for her and they sat down at the table.

"I want to figure a minute," said he. "Now that I have actual possession of the property, in place of a mere option, I can go at the thing differently. First of all, when I go up Monday I'll see my engineer, and on Tuesday morning I'll bring him down here with me. Then I shall secure permission from the county to alter that road and we'll build the dam. That will cost very little in comparison to the whole improvement. Then, and not till then, I'll get out my stock prospectus, and I'll drive prospective investors down here to look at Lake Jo. I'll be almost in position to dictate terms."

"Isn't that fine!" she exclaimed. "And then I suppose you can secure— control," she ventured anxiously.

"Yes, I think I can if I want it," he assured her.

"I'm so glad," she said gravely. "I'm so very glad."

"Really, though, I have a big notion to see if I can't finance the entire project myself. I'm quite sure I can get Dickson to give me a clear deed to that land merely on my unsupported note. If I can do that I can erect all the buildings on progressive mortgages. Roadways and engineering work of course I'll have to pay for, and then I can finance a subsidiary operating company to rent the plant from the original company, and can retain stock in both of them. I'll figure that out both ways."

It was all Greek to her, this talk, but she knitted her brows in an earnest effort to understand, and crowded close to him to look over the figures he was putting down. The touch of her arm against his own threw out his calculations entirely. He could not add a row of figures to save his life.

"I'll go over the financial end of this later on," he said, but he did not put away the paper. He kept it there for them both to look at, touching arms.

"All right," she agreed, "but you must let me see you do it. Of course I can't understand, but I do want to feel as if I were helping when it is done."

"I won't take a step in it without consulting you or having you along," he promised.

At that moment the bugle sounded the first call for luncheon.

"You'll stay for luncheon," she invited.

"Certainly," he assured her. "You couldn't drive me away."

"Very well, right after luncheon let's go out and look at the place again. It will look different now that it is —" She caught herself. She had almost said "now that it is ours." "Now that it is secured," she finished.

After luncheon they drove back to the site of Lake Jo, and spent a delirious while planning the things which were to be done to make that spot an earthly Paradise. Never was a couple so prolific of ideas as they were that afternoon. With 'Ennery waiting down in the road they tramped all over the hills again, standing first on one spot and then another to survey the alluring prospect, and to plan wonderful new and attractive features of which no previous summer resort builder had ever even dared to dream.

During the afternoon not one word passed between them which might be construed to be of an intimately personal nature, but as they drove to Hollis Creek, tired but happy, Sam somehow or other felt that he had made quite a bit of progress, and was correspondingly elated. Leaving Miss Stevens on the porch he hurried home to dress for dinner, for it was growing late, but immediately after dinner he drove over again. When he arrived Miss Josephine was in the seldom used parlor with her father.

"I haven't seen you since breakfast," Mr. Stevens had said, pinching her cheek, "Hollis and Billy Westlake have been looking for you everywhere."

"Oh, they," she returned with kindly contempt. "I'm glad I didn't see them. They're nice boys enough, but father, I don't believe that either one of them will ever become clever business men!"

"No?" he replied, highly amused. "Well, I don't think they will either. Business is a shade too big a game for them. But where have you been?"

"Out on business with S-s-s—with Mr. Turner," she replied demurely. "I came in late for lunch, and you had already finished and gone. Then we went right back out again. Father, we have found the dearest, the most delightful, the most charming business opportunity you ever saw. You must go out with us to-morrow and look at it. Sam's going to build a lake and call it Lake Jo. You know where that little stream is between here and Meadow Brook? Well, that's the place. We found out this morning what a delightful spot it would make for a lake and a big summer resort hotel, and at noon Sam bought the property, and we have been planning it all afternoon. He's bought it outright and he's going to capitalize it for a quarter of a million dollars. How much stock are you going to take in it?"

"How much what?"

"How many shares of stock are you going to take in it? You must speak up quickly, because it's going to be a favor to you for us to let you in."

"Well, I don't know," said Mr. Stevens, resisting a sudden desire to guffaw. "I'd have to look it over first before I decide to invest. Sounds like a sort of wild-eyed scheme to me. Besides that, I already have a good big block of stock in one of Sam Turner's enterprises."

"Oh, yes," she said, puckering her brows. "Are you going to vote your pulp stock with his?"

Mr. Stevens' eyes twinkled, but his tone was conservative gravity itself.

"Well, since it's a purely business deal it would not be a very wise thing to do; and though Sam Turner is a mighty fine boy, I don't think I shall."

"But you will!" she vigorously protested. "Why, father, you wouldn't for a minute vote against your own son-in-law!"

"No, I wouldn't!" declared Mr. Stevens emphatically, and suddenly drew her to him and kissed her; and she clung about his neck half laughing and half crying.

Do you suppose there is anything in telepathy? It would seem so, for it was at this moment that Sam stepped up on the porch. They in the parlor heard his voice, and Mr. Stevens immediately slipped out the back way in order not to be *de trop* a second time. Now Sam could not possibly have known what had been said in the parlor, and yet when he found his way in there, he and Miss Josephine, without any palaver about it, without exchanging a solitary word, or scarcely even a look, just naturally fell into each other's arms. Neither one of them made the first move. It just somehow happened, and they stood there and held and held and held that embrace; and whatever foolishness they said and did in the next hour is none of your business nor of mine; but later in the evening, when they were sitting quietly in the darkest corner of the porch, and Sam had his hand on the arm of her chair with her elbows resting upon his fingers—it didn't matter, you know, where he touched her, just so he did—she turned to him with thoughtful earnestness in her voice.

"Sam," she said, and this time she used his first name quite consciously and was glad it was dark so that he could not see her trace of shyness, "I wish you would explain to me just what you mean by control in a stock company."

Sam Turner moved his fingers from under her elbow and caught her hand, which he firmly clasped before he began.

"Well, Jo, it's just this way," he said, and then, quite comfortably, he explained to her all about it.